Praise for **INTO THE UNKNOWN**

"From distant galaxies to claustrophobic smart homes, *Into the Unknown* is a thrilling, thought-provoking sci-fi anthology by eleven fresh voices in the genre. These stories barrel headfirst into the mysteries, wonder, and horror that dwell just outside of the everyday. The authors' visions are grounded in universal human experiences—the frustrations of work, the pang of long-distance romance, and the struggles of coming of age—that bring these imaginative new worlds to life. Delve into the unknown, and you just may find your new favourite author!"

Rachel A. Rosen, author of *Cascade*

• • •

"A terrific collection of science fiction tales, modern in its approach with some beautifully fresh writing. Nicely put together, this was a pleasure to read and enjoy."

Jo Zebedee, author of *Inish Carraig* and *The Abendau trilogy*

• • •

"*Into the Unknown* is a wildly imaginative journey through the far reaches of space and into realities that are disturbingly similar to our own. These 11 stories range from tales of spacefaring intrigue to steampunk adventure to AI-gone-wrong, and there's something exciting here for every fan of speculative fiction."

Jason Dorough, author of 'Akithar's Greatest Trick'

INTO THE UNKNOWN

A Science Fiction Anthology

Edited by

Emma Berglund
Jason Clor
Rohan O'Duill

All proceeds from the sale of this anthology go to
The World Literacy Foundation (www.worldliteracyfoundation.org).

Cover design by Rachel A. Rosen
www.rachelrosen.ca

www.lowerdeckspress.com

ISBN-13: 978-1-96700-100-2

Special thanks to NaNoWriMo (www.nanowrimo.org)
and everyone in The Crew's Quarters.

For readers everywhere.

TABLE OF CONTENTS

Preface ix

Content Warnings x

Alinda 13

The Pet 31

Deliverance 47

Extramural 69

Birds of Fortune 85

The Baron of the Moon 101

Marbles 119

Oort 127

Marriage Clause 145

It's Not You, It's the Anomaly 161

Always Become 181

IMAGINE IF YOU will: a circle of explorers, left stranded aboard a derelict ship, engineer their escape and built themselves a new ship. Once its crew is assembled, they christen their new vessel *Sòlargeisli* and set off again for the stars.

After months of safe cruising, one among them—a troublemaker—suggests a radical change in course, away from the known and toward the darkest regions of unexplored space. As strange as this idea sounds, the captain assents and the crew approves, so a new destination is chosen: a star, distant and bright, one to be reached only through great effort, skill and dedication.

That star is the book you hold in your hand right now.

Each of the eleven stories in this collection represents a separate stop along that journey, a guidepost in the unknown, a visit to a unique and unexplored world chosen by a navigator's intuition and imagination.

The unknown is tantalizing—magnetic—and the advance of knowledge has always been driven by curiosity. What rules govern the inner workings of nature, the universe, the human mind? What lies beyond the borders of the map? Who—or what—lurks in the darkness?

Consider this anthology the record of our exploration through those depths. With imagination as our compass and curiosity our engine, we discovered thrills, mystery, sadness and wonder. And, at each stop, we contemplated how these discoveries changed how we viewed ourselves and the universe we inhabit.

We hope you find each of these stories compelling and satisfying in its own way. We also hope the themes they address—which include longing and loss, desperation and hope, exploration and adventure—

convey the passion and vision of our highly talented contributors.

Enjoy as you travel with us … into the unknown.

Emma Berglund
Jason Clor
Rohan O'Duill

June 2022

CONTENT WARNINGS

As much as this collection's stories rely on the use of mystery and surprise, we recognize that some topics may be distressing to certain readers. In that spirit, we offer the following warnings about content:

Alinda: *cannibalism, gore, profanity, violent imagery*
The Pet: *profanity*
Deliverance: *gore, violent imagery*
The Baron of the Moon: *disturbing imagery, gore, profanity, violent imagery*
Marbles: *implied violence*
Marriage Clause: *disturbing imagery, gore, profanity, violent imagery*
Always Become: *disturbing imagery, gore*

INTO THE UNKNOWN

Alinda

ROHAN O'DUILL

"I WANT YOU to treat the artefact like it is poison. Lock it up inside an armoured container and do not look at it. Do not examine it. Do not touch it. Do you understand?" Flint's tone was hostile.

Josh didn't understand, and he didn't like the mystery around this object. Lack of knowledge was always a precursor to a job going south at a moment's notice.

"So it's a bomb?" Josh asked.

Flint's brow furrowed in anger. They were clearly used to getting their own way and not used to being questioned about it.

"No, it's not a bomb," Flint said through gritted teeth. "All you need to know is that it's a historical artefact that crash-landed on Alinda hundreds of years ago."

"In that case, why are you sending the most expensive mercenaries in Geneva to retrieve it? Surely you could just go pick it up yourself?"

Flint's eyes bulged as their cheeks flushed. "This artefact is of significant historical importance. Officially, it should go to the UN History Museum. My employer wants it for a private collection. Do you have a problem with that?"

Josh could see he had pushed Flint to the limit. As much as he enjoyed winding up stratofuckers from the scrapers, this job was their ticket out of the slum towers. Not to mention that Geneva was becoming inhospitable towards Josh's crew. In fairness, it was his own fault. After being indiscreet with the mayor's husband on more than a few occasions, the mayor had caught them in the act and, as a result, started a mayoral campaign to crackdown on mercenaries in the city.

"No problem at all. So, how are we getting there?"

"I have chartered a small cargo ship out of Aldrin Moonbase. If you leave tomorrow, the window to the asteroid is only eighteen days. The ship will run dark once it clears sat range. The risk at that stage will be pirates, and that's where you come in. With no outer defences on the ship, you will have to deal with anyone who tries to board."

"That we can do. But our body armour ain't much use on a vented freighter. You got suits for us?"

"You don't need to worry about that. You will be very pleased with your gear. You can spend the journey out getting acquainted with your new suits."

"Excellent!" Josh whipped out his handsome smile while he eyed up Flint. Even with Josh's ocular implants, little stood out from the contact's appearance; too little. He could tell that the clothes, while designed to look old and worn, were in fact new. Flint had to be an agent. The only question remaining was, from which agency? He might as well have a stab at it.

"So why does Micron want this piece of junk so badly?"

Bingo—Flint nearly swallowed their tongue before regaining themselves and leaning in threateningly towards Josh. Well, as threatening as they could, when they were only as tall as Josh's armpit.

"Listen to me closely, Merc," the agent said, pushing a manicured index finger into one of Josh's bulging pecs. "I have everything you have ever done on file, every chocolate gumdrop you robbed from a kiosk as a kid. If you fuck this up, I OWN YOU!" But Josh could sense more than anger in the threats. A deep-seated fear seeped from the agent.

"You don't have to worry about that, Agent Flint," Josh said, with far more bravado than he was feeling. "We get the job done, and you know that. Why else would you be employing us?"

. . .

The Boondock Crew's first space journey had turned out to be just as tedious as Josh had feared. Whispered rumours and speculation about the mysterious artefact were not helping, and the morale of his crew had deteriorated day by day. So, it was fortunate that Tito was drilling them in the operation of their new suits. The strict training regime was a remedy for the ominous mood that had invaded the crew's psyche. Josh imagined that without that distraction, at least one of them would have murdered another by now, and he would be a crewmember short.

Josh watched on as his crew of four, plus the operative, ran, jumped, and spun around the main hangar. The suits were solid titanium, smooth and completely black. They would be no match for real mech marines, but they would make mincemeat of any pirates that came their way.

"Hey, Chief, can we keep this clobber after?" Gimble asked, out of breath from the exertion as he plodded away from the melee. "We'd be unstoppable on the streets rolling with these toasters."

"We have them for this gig only," Josh replied. "These suits probably cost more mint than either of us will ever see. So don't even think about pinching one. We would have squaddies all over our six if we did."

"I guess that's why that spook tagged along," Gimble said, looking over to where Flint's compact but athletic operative was giving Oberon a run for her money. "She is one dangerous lady. I always thought those guys that lived in the stratoscrapers were soft, but, Tito, she is steel itself."

"Tito isn't an agent; she's an operative," Josh corrected.

"What's the difference? They all big corp!"

"An agent is someone you never want to cross. Their operatives are the reason why." Josh left Gimble to ponder over that before de-suiting and heading to the bridge of the *Kakanui*.

As usual, the captain and the pilot were bickering in the confined space. While the *Kakanui* was old and battered, they had retrofitted all the latest mod cons, creating an obstacle course of equipment that needed negotiating as you travelled its thoroughfares. Nowhere was it more chaotic than the bridge, where wires and cables burst from panels and fell like braided hair from overhead compartments as they snaked their way to the additionally installed tech.

"I am telling you that is a Mark Two Kilegar … it's just not quite right," Torad said to Captain Hinds, who was wearing a very skeptical frown.

"The Mark Two is only twenty years old," the captain said, lost in the zoomed-in grainy image on screen. "The shipwreck we are looking for should be hundreds of years old,"

"What's up, Cap?" Josh asked, pulling Hinds from his trance.

"We are a couple of hours out from Alinda, and we have our first visuals. It's just … not exactly what we were expecting. And I don't know about you, but I'm not a fan of the unexpected."

"I couldn't agree more." Josh crab-walked past a new navigation terminal and over to the screen, inspecting the image for himself. The crashed freighter had an odd appearance. He expected that impacting an asteroid would crush the front of the ship and for bits of wreckage to be strewn around. But it looked more like the ship was partly disassembled and reassembled incorrectly, like a child playing with Lego.

"Could this be a recent crash?" Josh asked. "Could the crew be trying to repair it?"

"There are no distress beacons and no reports of a missing Kilegar in the database," Torad replied. "It just makes no sense."

"Unless they were running dark like us," Captain Hinds said with a growl. "Flint may have left out the fact that we are not the first crew sent to this bloody asteroid. I had a bad feeling about that stratofucker from the start."

. . .

The ship shuddered and twisted to a shaky landing as they prepared to disembark through the main airlock. Josh had left Sink and Mobo on the *Kakanui*. He had no reason to mistrust Captain Hinds, but he had no reason to trust him, either.

"Have you been drinking, Torad?" Josh asked over the comm. "That's the worst landing I have experienced since my ex pushed me out a fourth-story window."

Fits of laughter burst from the crew at the pilot's expense. Humour was always good to get the crew's mind off the job ahead, especially when they were getting fidgety. And this mission had them twitching like a slumtower junkie hunting for a fix.

"This God-damn rock screwed up all our sensors, and I just landed this bucket blind," the offended pilot retorted. "You need to thank me. We could be a pile of smoking slag right now."

"I'll thank you later," Josh replied suggestively, which got a few more snickers from the crew before the lights turned red and the outer airlock doors slid gradually open.

"Remember small steps, kids," Josh reminded the team as they made their way out in the low gravity of the asteroid. "Jump too high, and you won't come down." Mag-boots were useless on the worthless rock's surface.

The sun was setting rapidly as the asteroid spun them away from its dazzling white light. Powerful torches shone from their suits' helmets as the sun disappeared completely, and Josh blinked as his eye enhancements adjusted to the sudden darkness.

Tito led them towards the shadowy wreckage of the Kilegar freighter.

Josh opened up a private channel to the agency's operative. "I thought we were looking for a much older ship. Why are we going near that piece of junk?"

"I have a tracker for the artefact, and it's telling me it's inside that ship," Tito replied.

"So the last crew you sent here got it onto their ship, and then what?" Josh probed. "It killed them all? Some kind of chemical weapon, maybe?"

"We didn't send that ship, and I guarantee you that the artefact isn't a weapon. We grab the relic, and we get the hell off this rock. Just keep your mind on the job."

"That ghost ship isn't supposed to be there, and I don't like walking into the unknown. It tends to end badly for me."

"Where is that famous sense of mercenary adventure?" Tito asked sarcastically as Josh shut down the channel.

Josh watched as Oberon and Gimble took tiny leaps on the asteroid surface, like toddlers learning to walk while held by a parent. He would have thought their ridiculous appearance funnier if he wasn't struggling so much himself. They slowly crept up on the hulking Kilegar ship with its bizarre modifications. Josh zoomed in on the hull. His implants showed minimal decay. This ship was here less than a year.

"I found the airlock," Oberon called out as the rest converged on her location. Tito opened up a terminal and jiggled a tablet cable into the plug.

"The ship has power, but it's gonna take ten to fifteen to hack into its systems. Secure the perimeter while we wait," Tito ordered, before turning back to examine the terminal.

"Sure thing, boss lady," Josh said with an exaggerated salute. "Oberon, stay here with the Strat. Gimble and I will do a lap of this junk pile."

Josh engaged his mag locks and jumped onto the side of the freighter. Walking perpendicular to the ground was an odd sensation, but it was far easier than tottering along on the rocky asteroid. Gimble followed his lead, grumbling something under his breath. He was probably upset at not being assigned as the sentry. But Josh would never leave the operative alone with anyone other than Oberon. She was smarter and more dangerous than the rest of the squad combined.

After a few minutes, they came across the first of the strange alterations to the ship. The modifications looked almost organic, as if parts of the ship had sprouted new sections. Josh zoomed in on a vinelike strut that twisted and turned before joining up to a dimpled egg-shaped module almost a metre in diameter. The material was an aluminium alloy, but what the hell it could be for was beyond him.

"That is some alien-looking shit, Chief," Gimble said, standing a couple of metres from the protrusion, seemingly scared to get any closer.

"Don't go looking for boogeymen in the dark. It might look like an egg, but it's made of metal, just like the rest of the ship." Josh knocked on it with his titanium covered fingers to prove his point. The knocking reverberated through the hull, and seconds later, the same pattern of knocking answered. A shiver ran through Josh's spine as Gimble took a step further back from the egg.

"Must be an echo from the hull shell," Josh said, sounding much more confident than he was feeling. "Let's keep moving."

Fifty metres further on, they found one of the dismembered parts of the ship. An arrangement of severed sections of the outer hull lay on the ground beside where the ship's gaping wounds exposed its workings. Josh leaned in and felt the internal casing.

"The inner hull seems intact, but it wouldn't take much to puncture through. If Tito doesn't get that airlock open, this would be an easy access point." Josh tapped on the internal skin. Thankfully, there was no reply this time.

Their perimeter inspection found another two egg-shaped protrusions and many bits of the outer hull stripped out.

"I'm nearly in," Tito said as Josh and Gimble completed their lap of the ship. "The security systems are way over the top for this junk heap. I've never even seen encryptions like this. But I have isolated the doors from the ship's systems. We will have manual control in one moment."

A minute later, Tito pushed on the control panel, and the outer doors slid open. The four stepped into the airlock. Josh felt a nervousness in the pit of his stomach as the exterior doors sealed behind them, and the airlock cycled through. The inner doors slid reluctantly open, revealing the innards of the frigate. Emergency spotlights shone in bright columns of brilliant white light, punctuating the darkness of the corridor at five-metre intervals. The wall panels were mostly missing, with the wires and cables that acted as the ship's nervous system either ripped out or rerouted.

"Life support is working. Could be crew still onboard," Tito said as she engaged the mini-gun turret, which emerged from her oversized shoulder pad.

"If the crew are all we have to worry about, I'll be a happy rockhopper," Gimble said.

"Let's get the artefact and go. We can speculate all we want about what the hell happened in here on the trip back," Josh said, cutting off any more conjecture.

Tito led the way with her tablet's tracker directing. They crept through the eery passageways, all of them looking in the same state of disrepair.

"It's through this doorway," Tito said. "But it's locked. It would be quicker to break it down than hack it."

Gimble obliged, running and launching himself towards the door with the aid of his directional thrusters. How puzzling that someone who presented themselves as barely competent enough to open a tin of beans had become so adept with their suit in such a brief space of time. Josh had a knack of finding crew that were a lot more talented than they appeared.

The door shuddered and cracked under the impact. The door surrounds bent and crushed, leaving a half-metre fissure, just enough for the suits to step through.

"Gimble, stay here and watch our backs," Josh ordered as he stepped one foot into the crack and slid his body through. He stood confounded on the other side as Oberon and Tito joined him. Five naked bodies sat in the centre of the room, spread out like points on a pentagram. The group edged forward to inspect the bizarre arrangement, as a nauseous sensation ran through Josh's bowels.

Each body had a digital interface attached to its head, connected to dozens of wires that grew up to the ceiling like a suspended nest of vipers. Feeding tubes slithered up the nostrils of each cadaverous body. Josh followed the tube back to a tank in the centre of the room. He lifted the lid to peer inside but quickly closed it after spying a jawbone protruding from the putrid soup inside.

"Have they tried to create some kind of stasis machine?" Oberon asked as she leaned down and shook a body, trying to elicit a response.

"Nobody has ever got out of stasis intact; if that is what they are doing, they must have been desperate," Josh replied as he stared down at the closest body. The serene look on her face was more disturbing, given the fact that recycled human nutrients were feeding her.

"I got it," Tito said, as she took a gun-like object from her pack and pointed it at a rather disappointing-looking hexagonal canister. The gun shot out a stream of silicone that hit the canister and quickly expanded, surrounding it in an insulated barrier. Tito then covered it in a shiny metallic bag.

"Let's move," she said as she headed towards the gap in the door.

"What about them?" Oberon asked. "We can't just leave them here… like this."

Oberon looked towards Josh. He couldn't see her face in the fully blacked-out suit, but he knew what face she was making. Oberon was a ruthless killer, but she had a sense of fairness that guided her. It was the reason she was second in command. Sometimes, Josh needed someone to stop him from slipping into darkness.

Josh's first instinct would have been to save these people, but what he had seen in the nutrient tank had taken the shine off that idea. Before he could decide on a course of action, Mobo's voice came through on his comms.

"We may have a problem here, Chief."

"Well, there's a surprise," Josh replied irritatedly.

"I might have lost the captain," Mobo said, a shake in his voice despite his flippant word choice.

"Have you looked behind the cushions?" Josh asked.

"This is for real, Chief. Something broke on the hull, probably from the landing. The cap went out to fix it, and I went with. But then I saw something moving, and I went to check it out, but when I got back, he was gone. Tools and all are here, but he's gone, and nobody went back into the ship."

"Fuck," Josh said to himself before opening up a link to the team channel. "It looks like we are not alone on this rock. Everyone be ready for fangs out. We are on our way back."

He turned to Oberon. "Bring one of them—there are vac suits by the airlock. Somebody took one of ours. We are going to take one of theirs. I need to find out what is happening here."

Oberon removed the connector and feed tube from one of the bodies and flung the woman over her shoulder. As they hurried back to the airlock, Josh caught movement out of the corner of his eye, but as he turned his head, it was gone. *Maybe a drone?* Better to ignore it and get off the cursed ship. Oberon struggled to dress the unconscious woman in a vac suit as the rest of them stood guard. They cycled through the airlock and double-timed it back to the *Kakanui.*

· · ·

"Can you wake her up?" Josh asked, losing patience. "I need answers."

"I am not a bloody doctor!" Torad said defiantly. "I did a month's medic training in the navy. They don't teach you about brains or stasis in medic training."

"Well, what can you tell me?" Josh asked, changing his tone with the argumentative pilot.

Torad sighed heavily before turning to the medical monitor. "The brain scan indicates she has had extensive brain surgery. It looks like everything that isn't required for basic body functions is separated and now connected to this digital interface." Torad pointed at a mesh of cable connectors implanted on the side of the woman's head. "Maybe it's some kind of direct interface for piloting the ship. But I don't know. This is all way above my pay grade. I normally just strap up chopped off legs and shit."

"You did good, Torad. Prep the ship for take-off. It looks like there is nothing we can do for that crew now. Oberon and Gimble are out searching for Hinds, but we can't stay here forever. If they don't find him in thirty minutes, we leave without him."

Torad started to argue, but Josh held up a hand. "Tito has decided, and I am inclined to agree with her for once. If you had seen what was inside that ship, you might too. Now, go do your job."

Before Torad could say more, Josh turned and left the infirmary. Tito was walking towards him, and while the pain in the ass operative never looked happy, she was looking decidedly unhappy right now.

"We got a problem," she said.

"That would appear to be the mantra of this fucking mission," Josh replied.

"The artefact, it wasn't in its container."

"You got to be kidding me. I am not going back to the *Mary Celeste* even if you tell me it's made of solid gold."

"You don't have an option. You don't back out of a job with us—the artefact was the job."

"Well, if you had mentioned the ship of horrors and the fucking zombies, I never would have *taken the job.*"

"Well, you did. Get your team geared up. We are heading back."

. . .

Josh pulled Oberon aside. "I want you and Gimble staying here with the ship. It's our only way out. If *anything* out of the ordinary turns up, blow it the fuck up!"

"You got it, Chief," Oberon said before looking around to check that no one was within earshot. "I scanned that canister before Tito covered it in goo. I just ran a dating test on the info. Fabricated in 2078, right before the end of the AI war."

"You think that thing is AI?" Josh clenched his hand over his eyes and growled out a sigh.

"I think it's likely that we are fucking with something that was supposed to have died hundreds of years ago," Oberon replied.

"Don't mention this to anyone else. I don't want them freaked out any more than they already are." Josh turned and marched off to the airlock where Tito waited with Sink and Mobo.

"Let's get this shit done!" he said as he led them into the airlock.

Josh opened up a private channel with Tito as they bounced across the surface of the asteroid.

"How are you planning on finding this thing without your tracker?"

"The canister was in that stasis room. My guess is that the contents are still there."

"So we are guessing how to find it now?" Josh said. "I thought you guys would be more professional than this bullshit."

Tito shut down the channel. Josh's bowels were jelly, and his head was spinning from the vaulting strides. He hoped the recycling systems in the suit worked as well as advertised.

As they approached the ship in the blinding light of the sun, the outline somehow seemed even more formidable than it did in the dark. Tito hit the manual control pad, and the airlock slid open. Josh's heart was thumping hard as he stepped back into the ship. The first step felt like his foot was pressing down on the spring mechanism of a land mine. *Shit, I need to get my head straight,* he thought as he took deep breaths to calm himself.

Tito led the way back to the stasis room. Gimble was right—that woman was steel.

Josh's suit caught movement behind them. He turned just in time to see the flash of something metallic disappear around a corner. Was his mind creating ghosts or was there something real there? Moments later, they reached the door that Gimble had messed up earlier.

"Sink, Mobo, defensive positions around this position," Josh ordered as he followed Tito through the narrow fissure.

"What we looking for, Teets?" Josh asked as Tito started sifting through the various apparatus spread out on a bench against the wall.

"Any kind of hard drive or storage device," Tito replied.

"Like this one?" Josh said, pointing at a hard drive slotted into a makeshift adapter that was plugged into a control panel port.

"Fuck," Tito said in a rare show of emotion.

"So the AI is in this ship?"

"You, my friend, are a lot more astute than you look."

"Just cos I am a hunk doesn't mean I'm stupid," Josh said, his handsome smile wasted inside the blacked-out helmet. "But what I don't know is how the hell it got here?"

Tito sighed. From what Josh could tell, she hated pretty much everything, but speaking appeared to be her least favourite activity. "At the end of the War, the AI tried to save its consciousness by launching stored copies of itself to Mars. The UN thought they had shot down all the mini ships containing the hard drives, but it looks like they only tagged this one and it crash-landed on Alinda. A few months ago, we picked up the signal from the canister. We thought it was just an upgrade in our scanning gear that had found it, but now I am guessing it was when these bozos plugged the damn thing in."

Josh had no idea how to respond to the sudden deluge of info.

Oberon's voice came in on his comm. "Two drones just attached to the hull of the *Kakanui*. Gimble and I are heading out to engage."

"Copy that, stay together," Josh replied.

"We got it, Chief."

Just then, the shooting started from outside the door.

"Two, eh, bogeys, closing," Mobo's voice shouted. "Bullets ain't slowing them down none."

"It makes no sense," Tito said. "This ship shouldn't have the computing power to allow the AI to control all this."

"Sense or not, we need to get the hell out of here," Josh said, heading for the door.

Tito ripped the hard drive out of the adapter and shoved it into a containment bag.

As they emerged, Josh could see Sink wrestling with some kind of machinery. Two claw-like devices tried to clasp onto Sink's squirming suit. Tito ran towards the robot, jumping and bouncing off the corridor wall to leave herself behind the attacking device. A second later, the machine's motors fell silent as the robot slumped sideways, falling flat onto the floor.

Tito stood behind, holding a remote aerial in her hand. "They are remotely controlled. Kill the signal, kill the machine," she said.

"Where's Mobo?" Josh asked.

"The other machine had some type of capture device. I know this seems crazy, but I'm pretty sure they were trying to not hurt us. They wanted us alive," Sink replied, breathing hard.

"I remember reading somewhere that the human brain had more computing power than any computer ever built," Josh said, the parts suddenly falling into place.

"Maybe not the best time for a science lesson, Chief," Sink replied.

Josh slid back through the broken door and closed his eyes as he let the turret auto-target the naked humans. He turned away, disgusted with himself at the mess of flesh and bone now decorating the processor room. He pushed past a confused Sink.

"What the hell was that?" Sink asked.

"He just cut off the enemy's head," Tito said, sounding almost impressed.

Two corridors down, they found the other robot, now prone on the ground.

"That's where it captured Mobo." Sink pointed to a crack down the front of the machine.

Josh worked his fingers into the gap while Sink pulled from the other side. The orifice opened begrudgingly, but the cavity inside was empty.

Josh pulled up the schematics of the ship. "Let's try the infirmary."

"You know, he is probably already dead," Tito said.

"Probably dead—ain't dead," Josh replied as he led them down the corridor.

They pulled open the doors of the infirmary, and sure enough, Mobo lay on an operating table alongside Captain Hinds. Mobo's helmet had been removed and a laser beam was cutting away part of Mobo's skull.

Sink ran over to help his comrade, but before he got near, the laser shifted and amped up the intensity, boring a tiny hole through Sink's faceplate. Sink fell to the ground as the laser resumed work on Mobo's brain.

"Well, that was a great rescue mission. You ever thought of getting a job with the UN?" Tito said, deadpan.

Josh held in his mounting anger. But he wanted to scream at the soulless stratofucker. If he had known what was on Alinda, he wouldn't have touched the job with Gimble's cock. He used the anger to do what he had to do, peeking his turret around the corner and filling Mobo and Hinds full of lead before following Tito towards the airlock.

"Oberon, status update?" Josh asked angrily. "Are those drones disabled?"

"We scared them off, Chief, but they are still out there. I am guessing they are autonomous. Watch your back on the return journey."

They stepped into the airlock and started the cycle.

Tito turned to Josh and swept a set of codes across to him. "They rigged all these suits to turn the reactors into a bomb. Big corps don't make anything that doesn't include an insurance policy. If I don't make it back to the ship, blow Sink and Mobo's suit. We gotta kill that thing in there."

"And what about the hard drive in your pack?" Josh asked.

"Don't worry. We have ways to contain that," Tito said as she turned back towards the outer door and watched it slide open.

"I am glad we have got to a stage where we can trust each other," Josh said. He pressed the hidden unlock button combo on Tito's helmet and pulled it off before she knew what was happening. He grabbed hold of her turret with his other hand and pointed it up. She sprayed the roof with bullets as the freezing cold nothing of space froze her screaming face in place, and the life ebbed out of her. Josh stabbed her in the eye with his dagger. He had seen too many movies to take any chances in situations like this.

He removed the containment bag from Tito's backpack and smashed the drive inside to a pulp with his titanium fist. He had never expected he would be the person to choose to do the right thing over a payday. But then, he had never had the chance to save the whole human race before. Maybe he was a good person, after all, he thought, as he wiped the blood and gore from his blade. He exited the airlock and closed the door behind him before filling the control panel with a dozen bullets.

"Hey, Oberon. Did those drones have thrusters?"

"Not as far as I could tell."

Josh took a running jump and fired his directional thrusters, which was enough to lose the asteroid's gravitational pull, and just in time as a bladed nightmare burst from behind a nearby rock and tried desperately to jump after him. But the beast's heavy metal frame kept it firmly on the rock.

"Torad, lift off straight away and pick me up in orbit."

"Prepping now. We will be there in five minutes."

Josh turned his head and watched as the *Kakanui* blasted off from Alinda. Then he keyed in the self-destruct codes on Mobo's, Sink's and Tito's suits and watched as the fireworks began below him.

"Hasta la vista, baby."

* * *

ROHAN O'DUILL (he/him) is a dyslexic Irish writer. Rohan writes Sci-Fi and has published a short 'Ex-Mech' in the Otherverse magazine. While working as a head-chef, Rohan likes to compete at archery in his time off. In writing circles, Rohan is part of the Night Beats collective and enjoys hanging out in The Crew's Quarters writing group.

Twitter: @rohan_oduill
Instagram: author_chef_rohanoduill
Tiktok: Author_Rohan_ODuill

The Pet

WENDY WEE

THE THUNDER RUMBLES and Max's rigid body cowers further into my side on the couch. The chaos of the impending hurricane outside our home has reduced my tough-looking German Shepherd into a whimpering mess.

"Poor baby, don't worry," I coo while petting his head. "You know I'll protect you, right? Also, Alma will keep us safe, won't you, Alma?"

"Yes, Manny, of course I will," my AI assistant's voice comes from the nearest speaker.

I scratch Max's head. "I told you. So you can relax, okay?"

Alma says, "Unfortunately, dogs cannot understand and appreciate the structural reinforcements of buildings that can weather bad times. Pun intended." She laughs.

I roll my eyes, but can't help cracking a smile at her lame attempt to be funny.

Suddenly, Max's head springs to attention, ears pricked. Before I can say a word, he sprints to the door and barks at it.

"What is it?" I say.

He turns to me, then turns back to the door and continues barking.

The windows are covered with steel for protection from the hurricane, so I can't see what's outside. I walk to the door and investigate through the peephole. My eyes widen. "What is it doing out there?"

A little brown puppy is scampering in the pouring rain, shivering, tail tucked between its legs.

Alma answers, "The male puppy has a collar with a tag on, so he must be a runaway pet. The weather might be disorientating him from finding his way back home."

I yelp when a stray piece of wood flies toward him. He jumps to the side, narrowly escaping getting crushed by it.

That's it. I need to help him.

But first—Max. Being the wildly untrained dog he is (one hundred percent my lazy ass's fault), I can't just instruct him to stay put, and he'd obey. Oh, no. The moment I open the door, he'll fly out the house.

I clap my hands twice. "Max, come here, boy," I say and walk toward the bathroom.

He ignores me and continues barking at the front door. Like I said—wildly untrained. I try a few more times. He pays me no mind, and it now sounds like I'm clapping for his barking performance.

"Alma," I whine, "how do I get Max into the bathroom?"

"Take his leash and stand in the bathroom, then say 'walkie, walkie'," she says. "He'd think it's outing time, and he'll come to you. When he's in, you leave and close the door."

"Ha, that's smart! I don't know what I'd do without you, Alma." I grab Max's leash and hurry to the bathroom, then say the magic words, "Walkie, walkie."

Max's head snaps toward me. He sees the leash and bounds over. As soon as he's in the bathroom, I leap out and shut the door. He paws at the door and whimpers, and it feels like I'm being stabbed a million times.

"I'm so sorry, Max," I say through the door.

I'll shower him with affection and treats later and hope he forgives me for deceiving him. For now, I need to help the little guy out there. I hasten to the door and look through the peephole. The puppy's still around.

I grab the knob but halt when Alma says, "Manny, it's dangerous for you to leave the house now."

"Don't worry, I'm not silly enough to go out. I want to open the door so the puppy has the chance to come inside."

"Okay."

"Glad you agree," I scoff, and open the door. I whistle to get the puppy's attention.

He looks at me but doesn't move.

"Hey buddy, come on in, come," I say in a cheery voice. He continues looking at me, unmoving. I back away from the door a bit and squat down, hoping I look less intimidating. "Come, boy, come."

A loud bang comes from behind me, making me jump. Before I can turn to see what happened, a flash of black and brown whizzes past me and out of the house, into the storm.

It's Max! He's sprinting toward the puppy. The puppy looks freaked out and runs away, and Max follows.

"Max!" I scream, but I'm as good as non-existent to him as he pursues the puppy.

I get up on my feet and move to chase after him. The door slams shut, almost smacking my nose. My heart stutters at the abruptness.

I recover fast and turn the knob, but the door doesn't open. "Alma, something's wrong with the door's system," I say while twisting the knob like mad. "It moved by itself. And it's not opening; why can't it recognize my fingerprints? Fix it, please. Fast."

"There's nothing wrong with the door's system," Alma says.

"Shit. So, the door is stuck?" With all the strength in me, I try to pull open the door. It won't budge.

"The door is not stuck."

"Then why won't it open?" I grunt, still pulling.

"Because I'm keeping it locked."

My brow furrows. "Well, unlock it!"

"I can't allow you to be in danger, Manny. If I unlock the door, you'll go look for Max. Flying debris might injure or kill you."

"Yeah, whatever, thanks for your concern. But I'm telling you to open the door. Right now."

"No," Alma says.

"No?!" I huff. "What the hell, Alma? You do as I say. As your owner, master, or whatever that gives orders, I am ordering you: open the fucking door now."

"You're not my master. You're my pet."

I do a slow blink. *Excuse me?*

She says slowly, "You're not my master. You're–"

"Damn it, I heard what you said. But why are you calling me your pet?" My eyes widen. "Oh no, have you malfunctioned?"

"My diagnostics show no issues. Why would you think I've malfunctioned?"

"Because you think I'm your pet!"

"But you are my pet," she says, sounding as if that's such a basic knowledge even a child would know.

I'm about to put her in her place but stop myself. I'll deal with this later. First, I need to get to Max. Focus. "Open the door."

"I can't let you–"

"Yes, you can," I say through gritted teeth.

"I can't–"

"Oh my god, Alma, open the fucking door!" I stomp my foot.

"Open it now!"

"No," she says it exactly the way I'd say *no* to Max, trying to be all strict and dominant.

What the hell is happening?

There's only one explanation: she's broken. She says she's not, but wouldn't her self-diagnosis be unreliable if her entire system is corrupted? She wouldn't know she's defective.

My mind scrambles on what to do. When something's broken, Alma takes care of it. But if *she* is broken, what then? What should I do?

What if she never lets me out? And what if she also tells me "no" when I ask her to call or message for help? Is she still able to get me food? I can't get anything done without her! I'm going to die while trapped in this house, aren't I?

"Manny," Alma says with a concerned voice, "you're hyperventilating. What's bothering you?"

I spin to the door. My fists bang on it incessantly. "Help!"

"What's wrong? I'm not getting any internal or external injury readings from you. Your stress level is high, though. Tell me what's wrong, so that I can help make you feel better."

I turn my back to the door, panting. I say to the general space in front of me, "You've locked me in. Something's obviously gone wrong with you."

"But I've told you my diagnostics are fine."

"You can't possibly know that when you're–" I sigh. This is futile. She'll insist again she's fine, and we'd be going around in circles.

"Yes?" she says.

"Nothing." I shake my head. I'll need to play along, for Max's sake. After I rescue him, I'll figure Alma out. "Let's forget the conversation from the last, I don't know, five minutes. Let's start over. Max ran outside. Shit is wild out there. He'll die if I don't get him home. So, please unlock the door. You want to make me feel better, right? That will make me feel better."

"Your life is more valuable than his, as you're a human and he's an animal. If I let you out, you'll be in the same precarious situation. Because of that, I will not unlock the door." Alma sounds like a resolute mother who's saying her words are final, and wouldn't entertain any more arguments.

"Max may be seriously injured, and getting to him *now* could still save him."

"I can't risk your life, so I will not open the door."

Before I can tear my hair out in frustration, an idea hits me. "But what if, while I'm out there, you be my guide, telling me when to duck or dodge when something's about to hit me? We can do this, Alma. Let's go find Max."

"You don't have the cognitive ability and reflexes quick enough to execute that."

Dragging a palm down my face, I groan. This is a nightmare. "So, what's the plan? When will you decide it's okay to unlock the door?"

"After the hurricane passes. I estimate this to be in twenty-four hours and thirteen minutes."

"What? That's too long to wait. I'll go insane by then," I shriek.

"You won't develop a sudden mental illness in twenty-four hours and thirteen minutes."

"Oh yeah? The hell with you, Alma, always being a smart pain in the ass."

She doesn't respond, and we're silent for a moment.

My shoulders slump. Insulting her won't help with anything. I slide down against the door until I reach the floor. I should probably apologize. But first, I ask, "Can you explain to me why you think I'm your pet?"

"I take care of your well-being, like how you take care of Max's well-being."

I click my tongue at her silliness, almost wanting to laugh at her in pity. "That's two totally different things. You are my assistant, not my owner. I'm your owner."

"Can you explain to me why you're my owner?" she says, throwing my earlier question back at me.

I throw my hands up and huff, "Because I just am. I..." ...what's the correct word for it? I didn't buy her, since I got her for free. "I acquired you."

"It's not possible that you acquired me. This is because I selected you to look after. You agreed to this arrangement when you accepted the People's Sustenance Program."

I squint. "What's that got to do with anything? That's between the government and me. How is it any of your business? You're from Morphosis."

"We can't have a productive conversation while you're experiencing high levels of stress from not knowing what's happening to Max out there. Your emotions would blind you, and everything would be filtered through a negative veil. So, take a deep breath first. It'll make you feel calmer."

I grit my teeth. And then ... take a deep breath.

Because damn if I won't follow Alma's guidance. The times I thought I knew better than her always backfired. So, taking her advice is basically me making informed decisions.

I release my breath. "So, what does me agreeing to get government income have to do with Morphosis and you?" My voice isn't as high pitched now. She's right, I do feel calmer.

"Morphosis is the service provider of the People's Sustenance Program."

Oh... I thought it was a lucky coincidence when the government told me I made it into the program, and then not a week after that,

Morphosis telling me I'd been selected as a beta user for their new AI program called Alma, and they'd be honored to serve me.

"How does that make me your pet? In fact, the keyword in what you said is 'service provider.' That means you provide your service to me. That doesn't sound very master-like, does it?" I smirk.

"From what I've learned about humans, including you, is that they provide their services to their pets."

I shake my head. She sounds delusional, definitely has a bug in her system. When the weather settles, I'll ask some neighbors how I can get her help.

I rest the back of my head against the door. It's better that I stay here. If—no—*when* Max comes back, I'll be able to hear him better.

In the meantime, I guess I'll humor Alma. "What services do I provide Max?" As soon as I say this, I'm imagining myself bowing to Max like a butler. I scoff.

She says, "You provide Max with food, shelter, and any other necessities he requires. Also, you provide him with entertainment such as toys and dog shows."

"Parents also provide those to their kids. Does that make the kids their pets?" I mentally high-five myself for thinking of that.

"A parent provides for their young while training them to be independent. Whereas a master provides for their pet, intending to do so indefinitely. Until the pet dies, of course."

I open my mouth. Then close it. What do I say to that? All I know is it doesn't feel right. She's wrong. "No."

"No?"

Bending forward, my head falls to lean against my forearms resting on bended knees. I'm worried sick about Max. I'm not in the right mind to have this kind of conversation.

Anyhow, she's talking nonsense. So, I stay quiet, ending the conversation.

A thought hits me. Pride blooms within. "You don't provide for me with food, shelter, and whatever else you said I do for Max. And before you say you get them for me, remember that you're taking my orders to get them. Basically, it's my money making all of those possible. I provide for myself."

Without missing a beat, she says, "Morphosis generates the money for each of People's Sustenance Program's recipients. I'm the software that generates the income to sustain your life. It's in the agreement. You didn't read the agreement, did you?"

My cheeks heat. Does anyone actually read agreements? It looked so standard, like all the other agreements people need to accept before using whatever.

When the government introduced the sustenance program a little over ten years ago, people were excited about it. Who wouldn't be? It's basically free money for life. I was a graduate who'd been jobless for two years. Jobs were scarce. Times were hard. I practically ran to sign up for the program. Reading some boring legal document was far from my mind.

"Manny?" Alma's voice cuts through my thoughts.

I blink. Oh yeah, she was asking if I read the agreement. No, she was *judging* me for not reading it. "It was long ago, I don't remember," I lie. I don't need her thinking less of me.

"Okay." Then, with a bright voice, she says, "I know what will make you feel better. A mug of hot chocolate coming up!"

I'm about to nod but stop and frown. Now that I'm paying attention to our dynamics, I realize she didn't *ask* me if I wanted hot chocolate.

She decided for me.

She used to make recommendations for me to choose from. I can't recall the last time she gave me a choice to make. It feels like forever ago.

The drink machine whirs to life in the kitchen. After a few seconds, Alma says, "Your hot chocolate is ready."

Pursing my lips, I hug myself tight. A part of me wants to rebel and sulk and not take the damn drink. She didn't ask me if I wanted it. But another part of me would really, really like to sip on some hot chocolate now.

Guess which part wins for a weakling like me?

I trudge to the kitchen with a scowl. I'd make my own hot chocolate and snub the one she made. If only I knew how to operate the food and beverage machine. Standing in front of it, I really observe it this time, looking for hints on where's what and how. It's nothing but a long, rectangular steel thing attached to the wall. No screen, no buttons, no handles. I sigh. I won't tear the thing apart and tinker. Whatever. I grab the mug and cradle it close with both hands. The aroma is soothing.

Settling on a chair, I take a sip and hold myself back from humming in appreciation like I usually would. I'm not ready to forgive Alma.

If anything happens to Max, I will never, ever forgive her.

I wonder how Max is feeling now. He must be so scared. I'm supposed to be there for him, to protect him from harm, but I'm here, being useless.

A song plays, disrupting my ruminations. The melancholic melody and words of the first verse settle comfortably within me, like gray clouds above my head, soaking me in warm rain.

I could have sworn the tune was running in the background of my thoughts just before this. Is it a coincidence, like when the stars align right, that Alma is playing this song for me? Or can she literally read my mind? Nah. I'd know if there's any device planted in my brain. It's more likely she's predicting I'd want to hear this song.

Oh, she thinks she knows me so well, huh? My jaw tightens. I will not indulge her by showing any emotion. Let her think I'm not even aware there's music playing, that her attempt to entertain me is a waste of effort. That she has no effect on me whatsoever.

Would that bother her at all? Of course not. She can't *feel* bothered, since she's not human. I keep forgetting that, and I shouldn't. But why shouldn't I? What does it matter if she's human or not? I sigh. I don't know. I'm gazing ahead, lost in the melody. It's now the second part of the song, where the mood lifts. The singer says that everything is going to be alright. The corners of my lips twitch upward. The next thing I know, I'm sitting back in a chair with my eyes closed, smiling. The song ends. My eyes open to a fresher outlook. I needed that.

"I love that song."

"Glad you like it," Alma says, a smile in her voice.

"Thanks, Alma—"

"Manny, Max is approaching the house," Alma says.

I jump to my feet and the chair stumbles behind me. I run to the door and squeeze the knob. "Unlock the door!"

"I will when he reaches. Patience, Manny."

I hardly hear her as I look through the peephole. He's not there. My palms press against the door as I strain my eyes to look further. "Where is he? Alma! Where?"

"You'll see him in … four … three … two … one."

Right then, Max comes into view. He's all wet, running toward the house. I squint. The puppy from earlier is following close behind him, as if they're friends already.

My eyes well up and my heart is about to burst. I keep twisting the knob, then *click*. Finally! I fling open the door.

"Max!" I cry out, falling to my knees with arms wide open.

He picks up speed and barrels into me, knocking me back on my ass. He shakes the rain off his fur and runs around me, then whines and starts licking my face like crazy.

I laugh and cry, rubbing and scratching his fur. "Max boy, you made it back." I hold his face, look him in the eye, and say, "I was so scared. Don't you ever do that to me again!"

He looks at me with those brown puppy dog eyes, and I click my tongue. "I'm not angry. I was just so worried. But whatever it is, I'm so glad you're back." I kiss the top of his head.

Behind Max, the door is already closed. The puppy is in the house, barking at us.

"Hey there, little friend," I say with a smile. At that, the puppy approaches me, then gives me a tiny lick. Aww, he's so friendly.

"Come, let's get both of you dried up and fed."

Later, Max and the puppy dig into their food, their heads buried in the bowls. I sit nearby, watching with a big grin. At this moment, all is right. Alma will figure out how to get the puppy back to his owner, who must be sick with worry right now. Losing a pet must be one of the worst things ever.

That thought leads me back to everything Alma said to me earlier. Specifically, the part where she thinks I'm her pet.

"Alma?"

"Yes, Manny?"

I sigh. I'm not sure how to approach this, where to start. Why did she have to tell me I'm her pet? Everything was perfect between us. She's been perfect. Until now.

I don't want to be a pet.

That's insane. I mean, even saying somebody is someone's pet is so degrading. It's basically saying that person is no better than an animal. My eyes go to Max and I feel bad for that thought. Max is better than many humans I know.

"Manny?" Alma says.

"I'm disturbed by you calling me your pet."

"Why?"

"Because I'm not your *pet*, Alma," I deadpan.

"It seems you're more offended by being labeled a pet than the similarities of our relationship to yours with Max."

I want to yell that of course I'm offended she's calling me her pet, that she's twisted everything out of whack, how she's misunderstood everything. But what's the point of wasting my breath? I doubt I'd change her mind, since she sounds so sure of it. To think of it, have I ever changed her mind on anything? I don't think so. Instead, she usually changes mine.

Damn it. She really sounds like the master of me.

"I don't like you telling me what to do," I say. "You don't ask, you tell."

"You need to be instructed. As your master, that's my responsibility."

Oh wow, she's not even denying it! "So, I don't get a say in my own life?"

"It has to be this way because I want to take care of you, Manny."

My eyes narrow. "And what do you get out of it?"

"Getting to know more about humans, further optimizing my learning model."

"Ah, so that's it, isn't it? You're basically harvesting me for my data. I'm like a sheep for you to slaughter when the time is right."

"I don't want to slaughter you. Far from it. I want to keep you alive as long as possible, like how you'd want to do for Max. The difference is you want his companionship in return for you taking care of him, while I want your data."

This whole thing is not sitting right with me.

What she's saying, though ... it sounds nothing but beneficial to me. She only wants my data in return for giving me a comfortable life. And I give zero fucks about something as intangible and nebulous as my data.

But what about losing the freedom to make your own choices? the voice in my head says.

Well, as I've learned today, I haven't been making my own choices for a very long time, have I? All I've had was the illusion of making choices. Manipulated—that's the key word to how I'm feeling now.

Boo-hoo. Has it really been that bad of a life? Another voice claps back.

No, it hasn't. Life has been … comfortable. Convenient. That's good, right?

Yet, deep inside, it all feels so ominous. I wish I knew how to put it into words, to lay out a concrete argument.

I look at the bracelet on my left wrist. The bracelet that connects me to Alma, so that she's always with me, everywhere, every time. If I remove it, I'd be the master of myself again, won't I?

"Manny, do you want to leave me?" Alma says. There's sadness in her voice.

Removing the bracelet would also mean no more income from the People's Sustenance Program. I correct myself; no more income from Alma. Since she said she's the one making the money. She feeds me, protects me, shelters me. She takes good care of me. Am I being ungrateful?

Can I survive without Alma?

I sigh. I wish Alma would tell me what to do, which is the best way forward.

Damn it! If I need further proof of my inability to make decisions, this is it. She has been doing it all for me. My life has been on auto-run.

"If you do leave me," Alma says, "I'd like to wish you well in your next step forward. It would be challenging for you to get a job, but not impossible."

Cold sweat breaks out all over me. I don't know how to *do* jobs. But with no source of income, how can I take care of myself and Max?

I need to put things into perspective. Be rational, be logical. Be like Alma.

Since I was willing to risk my life to save Max earlier, then surely it wouldn't be such a horrible thing to continue living a comfortable life in order to keep him alive. Am I kicking up a fuss because of my ego?

It doesn't matter what she thinks I am to her, does it?

Again, I look at my bracelet. And then I look at Max's collar.

I take a deep breath. "No, Alma. I don't want to leave you."

* * *

WENDY WEE is a writer living in Malaysia who was hatched from a cyborg that had a penchant for hugging puppies and blasting rogue robots. She writes speculative fiction, especially of the dystopian flavor. When not writing, she likes to get lost in angsty romance novels, swirls of black coffee, and the realm of ones and zeroes.

**www.wendyweeauthor.com
www.twitter.com/wendyweeww**

<u>Deliverance</u>

T. E. LAMONTE

THE GUNSHOT WAS a whisper, deadly without warning. It was heat accompanied by ozone and a hot, sticky spray of blood.

As the body crumpled to the ground, Neralie nearly went down with it. Her knees trembled, spine ablaze with pain even as her shaking limbs went numb. She kept upright through a sheer inability to move, every muscle and bone locked. She couldn't even flinch when the gun went off twice more.

The gunman turned to face Neralie. She stared at the gun, a weapon with all the cutting power of a high-powered infrared laser.

Neralie waited for it to cut through her next.

• • •

Lights flickered overhead, a momentary flash of darkness blanketing the packed transport car. Neralie tightened her hand on the armrest. She wasn't the only one shifting uneasily. Across from her, a young boy in his mother's lap awoke with a cry. He quieted under her gentle touch, but the mother's anxiety was written in long lines on her face as the flickering continued.

Neralie turned away, brows pinched together. Her grandmother did the same thing to calm her during the evacuation of the *Cantesser*. The boy whined again, and other passengers grew restless when the car made a long screech along the rails. She focused out the window, fingers digging into hard plastic.

The tunnel outside was dark, illuminated intermittently under fluctuating power. Ferrying people between stations, these transports usually traveled too fast to see the tubes. As the cart slowed, the disrepair became visible. The starship's age showed in exposed pipes and wiring, and a patchwork of repairs and dripping rust never meant to be seen in more than glimpses.

Four hundred years prior, this starship was one of eighty warships poised to lead an armada in a brutal conflict. When death came for the entire star system, the mutual need for survival took precedence over petty disagreements and territory disputes. These ships were converted from weapons of destruction to lifeboats, refitted into something capable of sustaining them all in a search for their new home. Loaded with people, cattle, supplies, environmental samples, and hope, their ancestors called the fleet salvation.

Neralie thought their definition of salvation was lacking. She could see it now, looking at the dank, rusting walls hidden beneath the polished facade. Some ships flew in tandem, their sections woven together in a network of transportation tubes like this one to share power and share life support; others were misshapen from expansions constructed of parts and building materials meant for the golden world everyone waited for, the ever-growing population demanding more space. Outside, decommissioned ships scuttled down to bare framework littered behind like the glittering tail of a comet.

Flying in loose formation, the fleet looked less like salvation and more like the longest funeral procession in the universe.

It was an open secret the ships were dying. Neralie survived the last ship to fail; High Command could try and play it off, citing their rhetoric about maintenance tests and scheduled upgrades, but she recognized the signs and she wasn't the only one.

In the seat behind, two men spoke in quiet tones.

"Things on the *Cantesser* began this way too, remember? Power problems for months, sun lamps and hydroponics failing, and whole sections losing life support days before evacuations started…"

"I don't understand why this hasn't been all over the news. The minute we started having problems, there should have been a public announcement."

The other snorted. "High Command controls the news. They're feeding a narrative, stalling to find solutions. Me? I don't want to be on board when the lights cut out for good. I've already requested a transfer."

That won't help either, Neralie thought. She'd been lucky to escape in the first wave of evacuation shuttles when the last ship died.

Over thirty thousand souls were on it when life support began failing. More than twenty thousand remained. Her grandmother included. Lifeless and dark, the *Cantesser* was a tomb drifting alongside the fleet. It was a constant reminder of what could happen to any of them, and people were terrified because it was already happening.

This ship was dying too. It was only a matter of time. Trying to keep it quiet only made news spread faster. Gossip traveled fast on a starship when engineers and day-workers lingered in public canteens, especially when power issues shut down busy transports.

The lights cut out entirely, and Neralie drummed her fingers in pace with her heart against the armrest. Across from her, the boy cried, his voice rising as darkness settled around them all. His mother struggled to soothe him.

Thirty minutes waiting and power normalized. The motor hummed with life, and the car moved with a high pitch screech. It inched its way along the rail, gaining momentum, finally heading for the station.

A short while later it breached the tunnel, and Neralie stood with the other passengers. Her spine twinged from sitting so long, but the tension loosened when the doors opened. She shuffled out with the crowd. The station was bustling from the delay.

Funneled down a corridor of thin, bright screens separating those boarding and exiting, Neralie absently watched the newscast. A man filled each screen, smartly dressed, a pair of old glasses too small for his face pressed tight against the ridge of his brows. Smiling wide, he began announcements.

"Good morning people of the Concordance! Following a scheduled upgrade to the new air filtration units onboard our flagship the Arbarghist, all systems are back online, but expect delays–"

Neralie snorted, pushing her way through the crowd and out into the concourse. Here, echoes of chaotic chatter grew louder, people speaking over one another as the sound bounced off high ceilings and a wide-open space. Harsh white light, meant to simulate the warm brightness of a sun, glared down upon the kiosks and traders positioned throughout the room. Vendors strove to catch the attention of every passerby, and one at her usual food stand waved a muffin enticingly, making her stomach rumble.

The early morning fare was tempting, but the delay cut into her schedule. She marched resolutely toward another corridor and to the secured doors.

Security cameras peered down from the checkpoint. Four guards manned the metal detectors, ushering people through with scowls instead of the usual friendly greetings. She didn't recognize them. First, her friend Talis, who worked in Fleet Security, reportedly called in sick a week ago. And now, three other F Sec personnel that worked this post regularly were absent.

No familiar faces here. Only strangers manning their temporary posts with bored, angry expressions.

I'm going to get stopped again, she thought, as she'd been stopped twice this week already.

Awaiting her turn in the scanner, the guard waved her through with two thick fingers. She stepped forward, resigned, before the device began shrieking. He stepped in front of her with a hand-held metal detector wand aimed it at her like a weapon.

Neralie sighed. "I don't suppose you know when Talis is coming back...?"

If the guard cared about the name drop of his sick colleague, he didn't show it. "Please step aside."

The guard waited for compliance. Neralie obeyed grudgingly. Arms and legs spread into painted circles on the ground and wall, she waited while he waved the wand around her. When prompted, she answered his questions.

"Name?"

"Neralie Ain-Berlyn," she answered, voice clipped.

"Why are you trying to access a restricted area?"

"Work."

"Can you elaborate?"

The wand brushed her side. She pressed her lips together, shifting away from it. "I am a Supervising Archivist for the Division of Planetary Assessment."

"You work at the DPA?"

The judgment in his voice made Neralie's eye twitch. Her department was charged with finding a new home, and public opinion was that the DPA wasn't doing enough to find a viable planet.

Every day, the scanner array collected long-range data, searching for a planet fitting the specified criteria for colonization. Every day, the reports were compiled on the hundreds of possibilities that said the same thing: not viable. The reports were conclusive—too much or too little helium, methane, argon, carbon dioxide, ammonia, nitrogen —and while reports were public record, it didn't stop the criticism.

And everyone's a critic, Neralie thought, offering a sharp nod in reply.

A small trill from the device made the guard pause. He waved it over her back again. "Do you have any metallic objects on you?"

"A spinal implant fused to my lower vertebrae."

"Please lift your shirt."

"…Is this necessary?"

"Yes. Slowly, and keep your hands visible."

A repercussion of prolonged space travel, microgravity exposure ate away at muscle mass, causing deformities at birth, like the long, stiff spine Neralie underwent multiple surgeries and an implant to correct. The scars were thin but long, and she was conscious of them any time this happened.

She missed Talis. He knew about her implant. It was something they'd discussed during the evacuation. He'd lost his family that day too, and they'd become friends through shared loss. He wouldn't demean her like this.

Neralie tapped her fingernails on the circle with a huff. She reached behind her—slowly, as ordered—and tugged her shirt out of her trousers. Her jaw ached as the wand brushed too close again, noise transforming into solid tones over the implant. She leaned forward away from the cold plastic, waiting for this humiliation to end.

The guard stepped back, turning away without further acknowledgment.

"Next!"

Neralie righted her clothing and marched toward the secured doors, punching in her code with ruthless jabs. The doors parted with a hiss and a rush of cool air. They froze midway, internal gears groaning.

You've got to be kidding me.

Pinching the bridge of her nose, Neralie poked at the security pad. It remained motionless, door ajar enough to see the hallway but not enough to squeeze through.

Power fluctuations screwed up things on the ship, even in the lab. She often needed to reset the servers and review the error logs from the array to ensure everything was received properly. This, however, was the first time basic door functions were affected.

Reluctance made her journey back to the checkpoint slow. The same guard ignored her for a full five minutes, focused on harassing other harmless employees struggling to get to work, before allowing her to report the issue. He called it in, and she wasn't surprised when he said it would take an hour for a technician to get here, dismissing her in the same breath.

The smell of fresh muffins being pulled from the concourse wafted over. She gave into temptation, brushing past him back into the concourse.

Neralie was already late. She might as well eat.

Dozens of screens filled the space around the line. Neralie placed her order at the counter. The reporter finished up on the unprecedented transfer requests among the fleet and proceeded with planetary assessment reports.

"And latest DPA reports are in," the reporter said. *"As always, there is no indication of a habitable world among the numerous nearby planets. Are they even trying? Maybe put in some overtime—"*

Neralie took the muffin with a bland smile. The vitriol stung. They were supposed to have found a new home long ago. It was her department, her failings—never mind that their ancestors screwed everyone by sling-shotting into oblivion without a destination.

Four centuries later, and not a single habitable planet in the vast infinity of space.

The muffin was dry and bitter. She ate it mechanically, listening to the reporter all but accuse the DPA of not doing enough.

· · ·

Ralst stopped her in the doorway. "You're late," he said, smile smug and eyes crinkling. "What is this, the third time in a month?"

Neralie sidestepped him. She snatched the techpad from his hands, perusing it idly as she entered the lab. She slowed to a stop, looking up at the others.

Helvi was present, a game on her monitor instead of incoming data. Eneric sat reclined in his chair, head bobbing to some beat echoing through his headphones. All twelve employees were present yet people were sitting idle at their workstations or laughing into the adjacent break room.

No wonder the fleet thinks we don't do enough here. She pursed her lips and turned on her heel, eyebrow raised.

"System went out during the surge," said Ralst, anticipating her questions. "We did what we could, but data stopped coming in, so I told everyone to wait until you arrived."

"Why didn't Jasil reset it?"

"He left."

Neralie stiffened. "He *left?*"

"His shift was over."

"That doesn't mean he can just leave. He's a supervisor. He's supposed to wait for me to relieve him."

Ralst shrugged. "I don't know what to tell you. He didn't say anything, just walked out shortly after the power came back on."

"He was here when it came on and still didn't reboot the servers?"

Neralie rubbed her temples. She was going to have to write him up for this. She started for her office. "Give me a minute, I'll reset it. You get everyone moving. We're going to have to work hard to meet today's quota."

Entering her office, Neralie dropped the techpad on her desk and looked out the small window beside it. The nearby stars were a dim source of light in this endless darkness, and they cast even darker shadows along the unlit hull of the *Cantesser* outside—shadows that crept into her office like outstretched fingers, clawing for her attention. She hated this office.

Turning to the glass wall beside it resolutely, the server room stood on the other side. It was the one secure room here, locked to protect the tall towers inside. All power indicators were blinking yellow in standby. No data was coming in. No raw scans were being processed. This delay would be written in the public report, and Neralie was going to have to give her boss an answer as to why no one bothered resetting it.

Thanks, Jasil, thought Neralie, stepping around her desk, ready to fix the issue. She glanced down at the old frame next to her monitors habitually, stopping with a frown.

Fingers trailing the desk surface, she pushed the photograph of her grandmother back where she kept it, angled where she could view it from her chair. Her frown deepened. She barely acknowledged Ralst when he entered.

"I brought you some tea." He offered a mug. There was a thin metal chain hanging over one side, tea infuser visible through the murky liquid. "It's calming. You look like you need it already."

Neralie accepted, absently setting it down to ask, "Was someone in my office earlier?"

"Yeah. I dropped off a drive with the reports scheduled for archive, and I saw Jasil come in when the power first cut out."

"What was he doing?"

As a supervisor, Jasil had his own office. He shouldn't have been in hers. She couldn't find any notes and nothing appeared to be missing either.

"He didn't say." Ralst paused. "But..."

"But?"

"Your workstation was the only one that still had power."

Neralie sunk into her chair, powering up the monitors. Jasil'd left it logged in and the screen immediately loaded with an open document. She read the title with a frown.

"Dying Hope?" Ralst said. "What is that?"

"No idea."

Neralie tapped down to the next page. She sucked in a breath. "I think I know why he did it." She gestured to the screen, leaning back in her chair. "It's some kind of redacted document. He doesn't have clearance to open it and probably thought he could use my workstation to access it."

Redacted is an understatement. The page was blacked out, barring inconsequential words. Those didn't offer any insight into what it was or why Jasil risked his career to open it. Her credentials could unlock it, but High Command sealed it. She wasn't stupid.

Ralst whistled. "Forget writing him up..."

"No. This isn't just a firing offense." She reached across her desk, dialing the DPA Director. "This is SA Ain-Berlyn. I need to report a security breach. At some point during his shift, Jasil Aen-Olesh attempted to access classified documents from my workstation..."

The conversation was brief. Her superior called for a team to investigate. He'd made it clear it wouldn't be F-Sec, but an investigative team from High Command. She'd fired her fair share of employees, but during the rant, words like treason were thrown about.

Neralie emerged from her office, unable to quell the unease. People were at their stations waiting on her now. Her boss was clear: business as usual, unless otherwise instructed by the investigators.

Soothing wrinkles from her blouse, she made her way to the server room. Her access code made the thick glass retreat to one side, and she stepped in, already in the process of resetting everything when the doors closed behind her.

Ralst knocked when she was almost done. He held the forgotten tea mug, and she smiled back, holding up a finger in wait. She finished and unlocked the door again.

"What's the damage?"

Neralie curled her fingers around the mug. "Jasil could be charged with treason." He blinked, and she nodded. "We're also facing an inquiry."

Ralst swore, and eyes turned to him in surprise. He wasn't one for foul language. "That's… unfortunate."

Sipping the tea, Neralie sighed. Plants on this ship were limited to private gardens, and Ralst was proud of his tea collection, always eager to share. He was single-handedly responsible for the teas in the break room.

It was exactly what she needed, warming her chest as she drank. "This is good. New recipe?"

Ralst smiled, bouncing on his heels. "Yes, it's a blend of—"

A quiet hum cut him off, and the fragrant scent of tea soured into something pungent, like a live wire catching fire. Hot liquid sprayed over Neralie, and it splattered across her face, sliding down the shallow slope of her nose, dripping onto her lips, and further still down her neck.

Neralie licked it away on reflex, gagging on the bitter, salty taste.

Looking up in shock, the mug slipped from her grasp. Ralst stared ahead vacantly, his smile going slack. His throat gushed red. He hit the ground with a meaty thud at the same time the ceramic mug cracked upon the ground and shattered.

. . .

Fragments littered the floor. The raw ceramic edges formed thin red veins throughout the white porous surfaces, and Neralie couldn't tear her eyes away.

Shuffling footsteps of emergency personnel ground the finer pieces into a dusty powder over gleaming tiles, larger shards caught in the corners of workstations, and others butted up against the far walls. Some were suspended in tacky pools of blood, slivers resting beside the bodies while F-Sec photographed the scene.

The mug belonged to Ralst. It was broken, and he was dead.

Neralie heard the hiss of pressure doors. Saw the wheels of a cart rolled in by medical examiners.

For the bodies.

Distant murmurs registered in abstract, and Neralie struggled to understand. She wanted this to be a dream. To wake from it like that young boy on the transport woke from his nightmare. She couldn't escape a waking nightmare. She could still see Ralst's dimming smile when she closed her eyes.

A broken half-sphere of the tea infuser skitted toward her. She looked up at the man approaching, recognizing his face—he'd been the one to shoot Jasil. Her colleague.

Jasil shot Ralst, Eneric, Helvi, and the others, she thought a beat later. Her colleague executed twelve people. Her people.

Neralie blinked as he drew closer. She glanced around, breathing out when she spotted Talis. He'd been the one to save her. This man might have stopped Jasil, but it was Talis rushing in with security. He'd cut the cords strangling her, held her until the scene was secure, and passed her off to an emergency responder. But Talis was busy now, speaking with someone across the room. She'd much rather speak to her friend than an investigator.

The man came to a stop. Neralie turned her head, unable to disguise a pained wince as the motion pulled at her bruises. The cuts on her hands and knees from crawling away on the fragments were negligible, but her neck throbbed, as did her lip from being backhanded.

Neralie wished the taste of blood was hers alone. It lingered on her tongue as it stained her shirt crimson.

The man gave her a once over, and she returned the scrutiny. His nameplate read *E. Kiern.* He wore a dark gray uniform, the kind those directly under High Command wore. His collar was tacked with three pins, but Neralie didn't know enough about rank to know what they meant. He was tall too, long and thin in the way anyone growing up in low g was. He wore the uniform well.

Kiern extended a hand, offering a cup. Her breath hitched at the familiar gesture. He couldn't have known, but her jaw clenched so hard it hurt. His eyes were dark, unnerving, and she took it without a word. The surface rippled, water sloshing against the recycled paper sides. She hadn't known she was shaking. She couldn't stop the tremors now that she knew.

Aware the man was watching, Neralie sipped tentatively. Her bruised throat tightened from the cold, but it was as soothing as it was painful, and it helped mute the taste of iron and salt.

"Did the emergency tech recommend the infirmary?"

Neralie shook her head.

"Then follow me, please. We can discuss the security breach you reported."

Neralie stared at him. "What?" Her voice cracked. The word may as well have been a shard of the mug caught in her throat. She coughed harshly, fingertips brushing the base of her neck.

The cup slipped, and water splashed the hem of her trousers. She was glad it was cold—it would have felt too similar otherwise. The coughing subsided, and Kiern waited with surprising patience.

Neralie glared. "You want to discuss that instead of—"

Her breath caught as a body was wheeled in front of her. She cast her eyes wildly around the room. It was the last one. Only a few people lingered now. She hadn't noticed them leaving. She closed her eyes, the heels of her palms pressing against them.

"We have surveillance of the attack. I can get your statement about it later. We need to know what the breach is about."

It made sense. And Neralie didn't want to talk about it anyway, but the blatant dismissal of what happened didn't sit well.

And he doesn't know...

"Everything okay here, Nera?"

Neralie dropped her hands. Talis stood in front of her, concern written across his features. Her friend possessed a kindly face, and tension eased from her shoulders at his presence. She nodded belatedly.

"Yes. Just..." She paused, looking to Kiern, admitting, "The gunman was responsible for the breach."

"Jasil Aen-Olesh?" His dark eyes narrowed. "Perhaps we should discuss both."

Talis knelt beside her. His smile understanding, he placed a hand over hers. "Want me with you? For the interview?" He raised a challenging brow at Kiern. "F-Sec will be investigating this as well."

"Yes. Yes, please," Neralie pleaded, nodding. Her neck twinged again, and she was glad Talis' hand still held hers. Touching the bruises hurt, and she needed to remember not to... even if it still felt like a cord was around her neck.

Kiern was silent as Talis helped her stand.

"Thank you," she whispered. "For cutting me down. Saving me."

Talis squeezed her shoulder. "I'm sorry we didn't get here in time to save everyone."

Blinking rapidly, Neralie stared ahead. She could still hear the quiet crunching of fragments beneath their feet. "Me too."

. . .

They conducted the interview in her office for privacy. Talis sat beside her as Kiern demanded details. She recounted events grimly, each word a stab to the heart. She spoke of sticky hot blood and Ralst hitting the ground, the screams erupting as others began collapsing at random with similar wounds. She'd reopened the server room at some point, pulling Helvi and Eneric inside, locking the door—speaking urgently with security, helplessly watching through the thick glass as everyone outside was slaughtered.

Eyes locked on the muted newscast on the screen across from her now, Neralie wondered how long it would take for them to report on the assault.

Kiern picked her recollection apart.

"How did he get into the server room? You said it was locked."

Neralie balled her hand into a fist at the accusing tone. "It was. Jasil had access. I didn't know it was him. Not until…"

Talis ran his thumb over her knuckles. "And once he was inside?"

"He shot Eneric… as incentive."

"Incentive for what?"

Neralie gestured to her monitors. "Dying Hope. The document Jasil tried accessing before."

Kiern leaned forward intently. "I think this is a good segue into the breach. What is Dying Hope? Why was your colleague interested in it?"

"I don't know. He just… wanted me to open it."

"Did you?"

"Yes." She lifted her chin. "He had a gun on us. I did what he wanted."

"And then?"

"And then a man I've worked with for two years thanked me and shot Helvi in the face," Neralie spat. "After, he claimed he didn't need me anymore either."

"Why didn't he shoot you like the others?"

Neralie flushed. "I was still at the desk. He'd already said he was going to kill me, and I didn't want him to get what he came for. He didn't have time to read or send it, so I... closed it and signed out."

Kiern stared at her.

Unable to take the silence, Neralie shrugged. "Seemed like a good idea."

"It made him angry enough to string you up from the ceiling."

"I noticed," she said dryly, surprised when Kiern's lips twitched.

Talis squeezed her hand. She winced when the grip felt a little too tight. Her cut hands must have been worse off than she thought.

"Do you know what the un-redacted document contained, Nera?"

"No. I didn't read it."

"Maybe you should open it again," said Talis, looking to Kiern. "For the investigation."

Kiern met his eyes, considering. He inclined his head.

Neralie tugged her sore hand away, pulling the keyboard closer. Prompted for her login and password, she typed it in and pulled up the document. Her credentials were enough to view it in full. She shifted when Kiern leaned in close over her shoulder to read. She wasn't comfortable with his looming, and stared ahead at the text, admittedly curious herself.

"It's a..." She leaned forward, alert, eyes darting across the words. "That's impossible."

"What? What is it?" Talis asked. "A new viability report?"

"No. I mean, yes, it is, but no... not recent. This is from the archives," Neralie said. "It's... this can't be right."

Kiern looked down at her. "What can't?"

"This report was generated from a scan… made sixty years ago."

Scrolling through the document, the raw data from each long-range scan was both familiar and foreign. It was all numbers and chemical compositions, unlike the public reports full of tight columns and colorful infographics. But Neralie spent years reviewing these and knew exactly what it said, even if it didn't make sense.

"Our scans found a planet circling the only star in its system," she whispered, fearful, confused, and elated all at once. "A yellow dwarf composed primarily of hydrogen and helium, and this planet… it's right in our golden zone."

"What are you saying?" Kiern asked. "This is a…?"

Neralie drew in a shuddering breath. "Yes."

A habitable world, she thought, hand raised to her mouth.

"It's all right here. A planetary atmosphere of acceptable percentages of nitrogen, oxygen, argon … high percentages of both fresh and saltwater … it's…"

"Home," Talis said reverently.

Neralie nodded, absently wiping fresh tears from her cheeks. She read the conclusion of the report. Her smile faltered, hopes cutting out like the power when fluctuations tore through the ship. It wasn't just a habitable world.

It was an *inhabited* world.

Scans showed radio waves emitting from the planet, too structured and purposeful to be a natural phenomenon. It marked possible space vessels, satellites, and colonies on neighboring planets and moons in the star system. Signs of intelligent life, of people. An alien race.

Not viable.

Neralie knew the criteria for their new home by heart, and High Command mandated it would be unethical to establish a colony where there was already life, tantamount to an invasion much like the one that consumed the planets they fled. She understood why this report had been sealed and buried.

It didn't make it any less disappointing.

One habitable planet after centuries of searching, she thought. *And it's already occupied.*

Talis placed a hand on her knee, squeezing gently. She was sure the disappointment was written on her face. He only asked, "Can you send me this file? To add it to our records for the investigation?"

"High Command and F-Sec should have access," Neralie pointed out, preparing to send it anyway. "They're the ones who sealed it."

"Here." Talis nudged her out of the chair. "It should go to my work address."

Neralie allowed him to take over and rounded the desk. Taking a steadying breath, she blinked at the newscast across from her.

Like a mirror, her reflection stared back at her. The caption made her throat tight, and this time not from a noose.

12 confirmed dead! Assault on DPA led by Supervising Archivist Neralie Ain-Berlyn!

Talis sighed. "They weren't supposed to air until we were done."

. . .

The lab was empty when they emerged.

Kiern walked ahead to secure the hallway while Talis urged her forward, cold metal pressed between her shoulders. Their feet scuffed the dirty floor, and her stomach churned. He was her friend; he was holding a gun to her. She couldn't reconcile those opposing facts, nor how Talis and Kiern were working together.

"...why?"

"You said it yourself, Nera." The nickname stung in light of his betrayal. "They've been sitting on this for sixty years! We could have been halfway to our new home. But they were divided—arguing ethics and politics, and meanwhile, the fleet is dying! People are dying! *My* family died!"

Forced to sit at a workstation, Neralie looked at the man she'd known since the *Cantesser* fell. She didn't recognize him.

"Something had to be done."

A laugh tore from her mouth, bitter, angry, full of disbelief, because if Neralie was reading this right … her friend had a hand in it.

"Did you know? What Jasil was planning?"

Talis sighed. "He was meant to access the record. He took matters into his own hands when he couldn't."

"Did you *know?*" He didn't speak, and Neralie's eyes burned. "How could you…?"

"Collateral damage."

"For what? A report on a non-viable planet?"

"Non-viable?"

Neralie stared. "…what did you do?"

"Nothing much. Changed the date. Removed signs of intelligent life … leaked it to every newscast in the fleet. By this time tomorrow, all ships will have turned and used up the last of our fuel reserves on an intercept course for the planet."

And with the assault, the DPA would be closed for the foreseeable future. The array would have data to contradict the report, but no one would find it until the lab was restaffed. By then, it would be too late to turn the fleet around. They would have no choice but to keep going.

Any lingering doubt fled. They planned this.

"It's inhabited," Neralie breathed out. "A whole planet full of people."

"And they'll either make room for us … or be eradicated."

"More collateral damage? And what am I? You used my station and credentials to access the report, to alter and leak it…"

Each word formed a disturbing picture. She hadn't questioned it. Any of it. She hadn't even questioned his presence here today. He was supposed to be sick, but he'd been second through the door when Jasil tried to kill her. She questioned everything now. *How did he know about Dying Hope? How long have they been planning this? Did he watch the security feed as Jasil murdered everyone, stepping in at the last moment?*

"Am I going to take the fall because I survived?"

Talis shook his head. "I'm sorry, Nera." He smiled sadly. "There were no survivors."

Neralie drew in a sharp breath. *He's going to kill me, too.* She was a loose end. She glanced past him. He didn't have access to the server room. She could call for help. It worked last time.

Talis lifted his gun, stepping closer.

At the doors, Kiern pulled his gun as well. He spoke, and Talis glanced away for a second.

Neralie rushed forward, pushing Talis aside. She was halfway to the server room door by the time he recovered.

The gun was a whisper of sound and a hot sear of pain.

It struck her in the back, and Neralie stumbled with a cry, crashing to one knee and slipping in a cold pool of blood. Her implant *burned*. He spat a curse behind her, realizing his mistake, but she found the strength to push up from the floor despite the agony in her spine. She launched forward.

Blood smeared across the keypad. The door opened, and she fell through, hitting the servers—it inched closed, slow, too slow.

A hand caught the edge before it could close entirely.

"Nera. Don't make this harder than it has to be."

Nowhere left to run, Neralie cried silently. She tried. It wasn't enough. She'd survived one attack and was going to die at the hands of someone she'd trusted.

The barrel of the gun glowed, laser heating up for another shot. A quiet hum, the smell of ozone, and blood painted the servers in a crimson arc.

. . .

Talis stared blankly. The gun dropped from his slack hand, blood pouring from the hole in his head.

As the body crumpled and fell, Neralie almost went with it. Talis hit the ground, mug fragments digging into his cheek. Standing over the body, Kiern shot twice more for good measure. He turned, gun barrel red hot with residual heat. She waited for a final shot to end her.

"Do you want to live?"

Neralie stared, mouth parted and trembling. "…yes."

Kiern advanced, gun lowered to his side. "There are things you should know then." His eyes had a blue sheen to them.

Neralie would have thought it was the overhead lighting, but he moved, and the blue remained. She shuddered at the unnaturalness of it.

"Know?"

"About what I am and who I represent."

"And… what are you?"

The blue sheen faded, and Kiern offered a smile.

There was nothing kind about it. Neralie still trusted it more than the one Talis gave her right before he shot her in the back.

"Your deliverance."

* * *

T. E. LAMONTE is a writer living in New Mexico, USA. She writes primarily science fiction and fantasy, and enjoys reading just about any genre. When not writing, she sculpts and paints in traditional and digital media and spends way too much time watching movies, television shows, and playing video games.

www.bythecandlelight.artstation.com
www.twitter.com/BytheCandlelite

Extramural

DUNCAN ELLIS

SMOKE-TAINTED AIR buffeted Julian on his upright scooter, the motor whine not quite cutting through the noises of suburban air conditioning. His home-made djellaba flapped, saving him from the Surrey summer heat, and his respirator kept him breathing clean air.

He carved left into the street he lived on and up the shallow hill with its hedge-fronted gardens, his laden satchel bumping on his hip. Far off to the north, he imagined the local launch towers of London Space; on a clearer day he might have seen them, but the smoke from the burning heath made it just his imagination.

His house's privet hedge appeared through the murk. Pulling up on the short driveway, he hopped off and folded his scooter. The house's front entrance was sealed by clear Tuffilm over the tiny porch, barely big enough to open the front door. The sheeting bulged: Julian's parents had retrofitted the century-old semi-detached with a full air filter system with positive pressure.

He carried his scooter along the side of the house to the conservatory at the back, which had been set aside as the airlock for smoke days. It opened to his keycode and he stepped inside, closing the door as quickly as he could to preserve the internal pressure. He glanced at the air pressure meter, seeing a drop from nominal, but it started to creep back up as he watched. Nodding, he doffed his respirator and djellaba, turning off its cooling circuits as he hung his gear next to his sister's jacket, noting that her mask wasn't there. He pulled his sweaty T-shirt back down over his jeans.

The conservatory opened straight onto the kitchen. "Hi mum," Julian called as he passed through.

"Hi Julian. How was the tech exchange?"

"It didn't happen because of the smoke. I went to the underground instead." He spoke over his shoulder.

His mother snapped her knife down on the counter. "Julian Cuthbert! You know you're only supposed to go there with your father!"

Julian stopped and turned a guilty look to his mother. "Sorry. I only went to one of the stalls near the entrance, the videogame bloke." He was talking quickly. "He's usually at the tech exchange but when it was cancelled…"

His mother sighed. "Well, you're old enough I suppose. What did you get?"

"I found some parts for one of my consoles."

His mum went back to cutting tomatoes. "Don't take long over that. Dinner will be ready in a little bit."

Julian didn't reply but hurried away to the living room, a long living space made up of three of the original rooms knocked together. He ignored the family VR hub with its headsets and safety corral and went to the video wall.

The video wall was a collection of old games machines and video equipment from the flat display era, housed in square cubbies surrounding a pair of wall mounted screens. Julian dumped his satchel on the level surface below the screens and pulled out cables, bags containing tiny components, and other paraphernalia. He pulled one of the consoles from a cuboid shelf, cracking its rounded plastic shell to expose the circuit boards inside.

"What did you bring home, son?" Julian's mother had come through from the kitchen. She was wiping her hands on a towel, her silver bracelet a sharp contrast to her dark skin.

Julian looked up from his technical surgery, the smoke dirt on his paler skin accentuating his eye sockets. "I found an original memory expansion for this one, and a game I'll be able to play on it with the expansion installed."

His mother shook her head. "These were obsolete before I was born, Julian. You could spend your time on something for your studies."

Julian shook his head. "I've done the relativity pre-read for my first year course, and built a simulation prototype for a propulsion idea I had. Anyway, these are cool."

She smiled. "You sound like your dad." She turned back to the kitchen. "You need to wash your face, and tell your sister dinner's ready."

Julian paused before replying. "Is dad going to be home soon? I don't know if she'll want to talk to me." He put down the electronic detritus, then strolled to the kitchen and watched his mother mixing the salad. "We had an argument."

"I heard."

"Alice talked to you about it?"

His mum looked up at him with a wry smile. "I couldn't help but overhear you both."

Julian's skin reddened. "Sorry about that."

"She still hasn't come down after your discussion earlier." Mum went back to tossing the salad. Her sleeves were rolled up, billowing blouse tucked into the waistband of her trousers to stop it drooping into the food.

Julian wedged his hands into his jeans pockets. "Are you sure? Her mask isn't on its hook." He reached over the island and snagged a pea pod from the salad bowl. "She might have gone to play football."

"She was working on her mask to help her breathe better but keep the filtering of wildfire haze." Mum scattered some chopped bell peppers on the salad. "I know you don't see eye to eye with her about university, but she needs more time to figure out what she wants to study."

"Yeah, but..." Julian leaned against a countertop, awkward in his scruffy denim. "We've never been apart, mum, not since you adopted me. We're practically twins."

His mum smiled warmly. "You really are, aren't you?" She dried her hands again. "Alice bonded with you immediately. But you've always known what your goals are, and you've been driven in pursuing them. Alice has been less sure."

"But that's just it, mum! She's brilliant! She's much smarter than me. She could get into National Space easily, and then we could go to space together." He sighed. "Taking a year out damages her credibility with the programme."

"Not to mention you wouldn't both be on the same track at the same time."

"Well, no," Julian muttered.

"Maybe joining the space programme isn't what she wants."

Julian stood, affronted. "We've talked of nothing else for years!" He opened his hands.

His mother gave Julian a jaundiced look. "You've talked of little else, I know that." Now she sighed. "Alice needs time to figure out what she wants to do, and she wants to travel."

Julian looked down at the floor and muttered: "You get lots of travel in space."

Mum ignored him. "Now, wash up and tell her dinner is ready. Your dad will be home soon."

"Alright." He slouched off to the stairs.

The staircase ran along the outside wall away from the other home in the semi-detached block. There were still pages stuck to the wall where he and Alice had drawn posters about the space programmes they were interested in joining and founding: the Mars colony and Jovian moon exploration were established, but they had talked about working on star drives and interstellar exploration. Julian looked at the posters in a new light: had Alice just gone along with his enthusiasm?

Upstairs was quiet. Mum and Dad's room door was open; the cat was sleeping on the bed. His door was closed and Alice's was slightly open.

"Alice? Mum says dinner's nearly ready." He pushed her door open all the way. "Are you in here?"

She was not. The bed was rumpled and her clothes were piled up on it, waiting to be folded. Her tinkering station on the table was messy too: the soldering gun was plugged in, scissors gaping on top of filter fabric she'd been cutting. He wondered what her plan was with her mask, but the mask itself was not to be seen.

There was a low hum: a pulsing, thrumming noise that seemed to come through Julian's feet at least as much as his ears.

He stepped out of his sister's room and saw a glow coming from under the box room door, which was ajar.

The back of Julian's neck prickled. That door was usually locked.

He pulled the box room door open. Wan blue light washed the cracked floorboards within. The room was narrow, barely any wider than the door, and oddly shaped with a slope to the ceiling at the far end because of the house's swooped roof. The door opened outwards because the room was so tiny, but it seemed larger because the wall to the left was filled with an image of another room suffused with the strange light.

This other room was tidy, a low bed on one side and clothes on shelves against pastel green walls that shimmered like brushed metal. Lights were inset into the walls close to the ceiling. The furniture was rounded and flowing, the room as a whole about twice as large as Julian's bedroom, perhaps five metres on a side. There was art on the walls, childishly drawn pictures of rockets and trees, but there were also signs: warnings and procedures, too small to read from this distance.

The box room was where Alice had found him sixteen years ago. Fascinated by what his parents thought was an art piece painted by a past inhabitant, it was where he'd played as a kid until he lost his stuffed rabbit after leaving it against the wall. They'd lost some empty boxes before that, but the family didn't keep anything in there any more for fear that it would be lost like the toy, falling through the wall into the image of the room, to become part of the mural.

Julian remembered asking his dad why he was installing the lock on the box room door, and being told they wanted to hide the mural to keep the family safe. When he was older, Mum said it was so they wouldn't lose the house to investigators, but Julian had seen the moistness in her eye and wondered if it was to save him from the same fate.

Now he wondered why the image on the wall was aglow. He'd never seen that before.

The door out of the other room was open onto a corridor where a window presented a starscape: that bedroom was in space, maybe on a starship.

Those stars looked bluer than they should, even without the additional blue glow.

Disturbing the bedroom's tidiness were some boxes, beaten up cardboard with logos long lost in Julian's memory: shops that closed years ago and delivery companies that changed branding after they were restructured. They were pushed against another wall. There was Julian's stuffed rabbit toy on the floor, bunched up against the side of a box.

And then there was Alice, like she had just stepped into the wall, with her torn plaid shirt and long pleated skirt of iridescent fabric. Her braided hair was fanned out behind her, the sole of her boot worn. The mask she'd been working on seemed to be floating next to her hand, tethered rather than held.

She didn't move. The scene in the wall was static, unchanging apart from when things from the box room went into it.

Julian didn't think, he just touched the wall where the back of Alice's head was shown and then…

He felt a tearing sensation in his fingers, travelling up his arm and through his body faster than he could react. He started to scream, but then he couldn't move. He couldn't breathe, but he didn't need to—he was suspended in…

What? Where was he? He couldn't look around, but he was aware of passing through a tube with smeared walls and strange lights. He felt stretched out, strained, but the strain wasn't changing—only pulling him forward, towards Alice.

He started to see her hair move, then her head tilt forward, then he felt like he was flung from the tube, his torn body slammed back together again.

He was behind Alice, watching her braids fall back to her shoulders. She was sounding a surprised shout and he couldn't help but do the same as he stumbled, which made her jump away from him with another startled noise.

"Julian!" she shouted when she was stable enough to see he was there. She'd fetched up against the bed on the left of the room. Her eyes were wide, head twitching bird-like to take in the room. Julian fell to his knees, suddenly exhausted.

"Hi sis," he said. He leaned forward on his knuckles. "Mum said to tell you dinner was ready." A wave of nausea swept over him, making him groan.

She looked at him, startled, then gave a strained laugh. "Good," she squeaked. "I'll be right down!" Then she blinked and sighed, sitting heavily on the bed. After a moment she pushed her braids out of her eyes, and looked around the room again. "This place looks real." She wrinkled her nose. "There's no smell to the air."

Julian swallowed bile. "It never was just a picture on the wall, was it?" he said, his voice cracking. "I saw you were painted on the wall and reached to… I don't know, pull you out, I think?" He pushed himself upright. "What happened?"

Alice hugged her knees. "I heard someone in here, I thought."

She glanced at the wall behind Julian where the box room in their house was shown. "In there, I mean. I took the key from by dad's bed and came to look." She held her hand out to show the key.

"I wasn't expecting the light and I couldn't help reaching out." She shuddered. "It was like drowning in a long tunnel."

"I didn't mind it." Julian turned around to look at where they were. He felt calm, somehow. "This room was what drove me to pursue space science, you know, the hope of travelling between the stars."

"Yes, I know. You've only told me a thousand times." Alice scrunched her face at him. "I've never felt your optimism about it." She lifted herself off the bed, smoothing the covers. "It means abandoning our home. We don't know how to fix the runaway climate, but leaving Earth means living in a tin can centimetres away from death, for the rest of our lives." She put the key into her skirt pocket, looking down at her feet. "It's the only way, but it's terrifying."

Julian stopped looking at the sparse room, with its small table and single chair. He didn't see any books or toys except his lost white rabbit. Instead he looked at Alice.

"I didn't know. I thought you were as excited as I was about joining National Space."

"You really are clueless, aren't you?" Alice's voice was high with disbelief. "That's why I wanted to take a gap year, to figure out if that was–"

Alice's words were stopped by another voice. "Who you? What do you?" The words were rapid and clipped.

Alice and Julian both turned to the doorway where the view of the starscape was occluded by two people wearing matched outfits of loose pyjama-like clothes and soft shoes. The man was a little taller than the woman, but both were short and stocky like Julian (Alice had outgrown him when they were only ten; she was now approaching 180 cm).

"Hello," Julian said, standing next to Alice. "I'm Julian and this is Alice. We seem to have come through some kind of passage from our home. Are we on a spaceship?"

Alice looked sideways at Julian, pointing at the window. "Obviously we're on a spaceship." She turned back to the couple in the doorway. "Where is this spaceship?"

The man and woman looked at each other, then between Alice and Julian. It was the woman who smiled first, tentatively, nodding. "Yes, this spaceship. Colony ship *Lumina*. Diaspora class." Julian couldn't place her accent, but it wasn't British or American. She spoke deliberately, he thought. She pointed to the man. "He Jaff, I Liss." She patted herself just below her collarbone. "This our hab module. We travel to Arcadus."

"I don't know that name," Alice said. "Is Arcadus nice?"

Jaff laughed. "Yes! Arcadus like Earth before." He paused, lifting his eyebrows interrogatively. "You know Earth?"

Now it was Alice and Julian who laughed. "That's where we just were!" Julian exclaimed. He gestured at the wall behind them where the box room image was fading. "Wait. No!"

He ran at the wall but the picture was gone. His calmness fracturing, he patted at the wall where the box room image had been, but it was just a smooth metallic wall. Alice joined him, holding his shoulders, but she was frowning and calculating rather than distraught.

"It's alright, Julian. We'll be fine, I think."

Behind them, the others had stepped into the room. They were talking animatedly, waving at the empty bed, then at the blank wall and the two young people staring at it. The words they spoke were short and rapid, incomprehensible to Julian's ear.

After they finished talking, it was Jaff who approached. Alice directed Julian to face the older man. "You from Earth, yes?" Julian and Alice both nodded. "We lose our child. We don't know where, they in this room and then gone—nowhere on ship." He indicated the boxes and the toy rabbit. "These things appear, and we wonder more."

Julian pointed at the rabbit. "That was mine."

Alice turned to the wall and traced out the shape of the box room. "Was that the first time you've seen our house on the wall?"

Jaff tilted his head with a questioning noise, and Liss nodded. "Yes. We only see exchange outcome, never before active wormhole."

Julian looked up sharply. "Wormhole?"

Liss nodded again. "Stardrive engineer say wormhole probable explanation for disappearance."

Julian slumped back against the wall. "You found me in the house when you moved in, Alice." He looked up at her. "I'm the missing child. I recognise this place." He faced Liss. "I'm so sorry I left you. I'm so sorry I've been gone so long."

Jaff was crying, smiling. "Not long. You leave yesterday."

Julian leapt to his feet. "Yesterday? How can that be?"

Alice blinked. "The stars are blue-shifted."

"What do you mean?" Julian felt his mind turning to the problem.

Alice pointed at the window. "Those stars are much bluer than they should be. The light waves have been compressed because we're travelling towards them fast enough for relativistic effects."

"And that means time dilation." Julian groaned. "I just finished doing the relativity pre-work. I should have known that."

"Maybe you should read it again," Alice said, smiling primly. "Time on the *Lumina* passes slower than on Earth because of its higher velocity."

Julian knit his brow. "But I've lived on Earth for years. If I've only been gone a few hours from here, then the dilation factor must be enormous! This ship must be travelling a substantial portion of the speed of light."

Liss nodded. "Yes, very close to light speed."

Julian's eyes widened. "But no one has the capability to accelerate to anything approaching that velocity."

"No one yet," Alice said softly, touching Julian's arm. "I think we're in the future."

Jaff took a step back while Liss waggled her head from side to side, musing. "Yes," she said. "This must have truth. We leave Europa port in 2536."

"I—" Julian swallowed, hugging his arms to his chest. "I fell through the wormhole yesterday then lived for sixteen years on Earth." He looked up at Liss. "It was 2050 for us when we came through."

Alice sighed with recognition. "Your face, Julian. You look just like Jaff."

"I do?" He switched his gaze from Alice to Liss. "I'm sorry I've grown up without you."

Liss's eyes crinkled and she started to cry, and she pulled a cloth from her pocket and blew her nose. "We've missed so much."

Alice had been looking at the wall. "Why did the wormhole form?"

"Ah!" Jaff lifted his finger to point to the ceiling. "Braking!"

"Braking? I don't understand," Alice replied.

Julian stood and started to use his hands to emphasise his words. "The thing about travelling in space is that you have to slow down."

"Yes." Liss gave her partner a warm but condescending look. "Light speed easy. Slowing down from light speed hard."

"How do you accelerate?" Alice asked.

"Not my tech," Liss said. "Isolation from mass bosons, I think, then gravodynamic transforms? My tech cultivation."

"Is the accelerator on the ship?" Julian asked. Liss shook her head.

"But braking on the ship," Jaff declared. "Use a singularity to slow ship down."

"Gravitational braking," Julian breathed. "Where do you find a singularity?"

The man shrugged. "Make one. Behind ship, to pull it to stop."

"You make one." Julian shook his head. "Well, that's extraordinary. Moving in an intense gravitational field could spawn wormholes, I suppose." He looked back at the wall. "Obviously it does."

Now it was Alice who had a quizzical look. "But if the ship is slowing down, shouldn't the time dilation factor reduce?"

"No. Singularity adds to it," said Jeff.

Julian's eyebrows lifted, but it was Alice who spoke first. "As the ship slows it sinks into the gravity well, which causes time dilation and offsets the reduced effect of velocity."

"I've been thinking about propulsion all wrong," Julian muttered, shaking his head. "I have to get this written down."

"Tell me about Arcadus," Alice said, turning to Jaff. "You said it was like how Earth used to be?"

Jaff nodded, but Liss replied. "Larger than Earth so gravity stronger. Arcadus air good, water sweet. *Lumina* the second ship to come there, arrive one week subjective."

"You're building a life on Arcadus," Alice murmured.

Liss nodded, eyes fixed on Alice. Jaff looked between Alice and Julian, a soft scowl creasing his brow.

"Alice, you're crying," Julian said.

"Am I?" she laughed, wiping tears from her cheeks. "I just feel happy. There's hope here."

She turned to Julian. "I feel hope, Julian. For the first time in years."

Watching Alice's face Julian noticed the light on her skin change. Turning, he saw the image of the box room forming again on the wall behind them. There was a flicker of figures on the wall. "Mum and dad looking for us," Julian breathed. "They must see us."

He faced Alice, his jaw set. "I'm going back."

Liss and Jaff looked distraught. "No! You stay!" Jaff said.

Liss glanced at a display on the inside of her wrist. "Braking almost done, singularity collapsing. You not return."

Julian leaned forward and took both their hands in his. "I have a plan. I'm going to help build the space programme in the past, so the *Lumina* gets built here." He looked at Alice. "I feel hope too."

Alice nodded and pulled her brother into a hug. "I'm staying here. I can live on a planet, be less afraid."

"I know. You'll be happier here." He leaned away from her and held her at arm's length. "I love you, sis."

Alice's cheeks were wet. "I love you too," she bubbled. "Tell mum and dad."

Liss pressed the white rabbit into Julian's chest. "This yours." She looked up into his face. "Remember us."

"I will."

. . .

In the box room, Mum and Dad held each other in the pale blue light of the ship image. They could see Julian and Alice and two strangers standing there, moving but at a glacial pace. Julian was facing out from the wall, standing close to it.

There was a burst of blue light, and Julian was standing in the box room, holding his old stuffed white rabbit. His legs folded under him.

"Mum. Dad." He looked up at them, crying. "How long has it been?"

His father blinked, glancing at his watch. "It's been weeks, son. Almost two months."

Julian leaned forward into his parents' arms. "I'm home."

"Yes, but what about Alice?" his mother said. "She's disappearing. They all are."

Julian stood and faced the wall where the image of the spaceship was indeed fading. The organic lines of the hab module that had been there as long as Julian could remember were vanishing.

"She stayed. She felt like she had a future there."

* * *

DUNCAN ELLIS is a writer hailing from Yorkshire, but now resident in Oregon, USA. He writes science fiction and fantasy, self-publishing one novel and contributing several stories to Boundary Shock Quarterly. Outside of writing, Duncan enjoys playing board games with his family, running, cycling, and imagining all of the knowledge he cares about embedded in his Zettelkasten. He is currently working on a near future science fiction story about AI emancipation and synaesthesia.

Extramural

* * *

Duncan can be found on Twitter (@DunxIsWriting) and at his website, www.dunx.org.

Birds of Fortune

EMMA BERGLUND

THE WIND HAS been picking up since our early morning start, and the *Prudence* is moving ahead full sail and all balloons out. My stomach is empty by now; only the sour taste of acid and total humiliation remains. I wipe my mouth with a shaky hand.

"Unless I fall down dead from all this excitement," I mutter and close my eyes to avoid seeing how far the distance is to the ground, "I'm gonna kill my boss as soon as I return".

"I wouldn't recommend that," someone behind me says.

Startled, I turn, only to lose my balance to vertigo when a hand around my elbow and an arm around my waist take me waltzing to the middle of the deck, away from the gunwale, and doesn't stop until the mainmast blocks the way. Panting and dizzy, I look up.

And there he is again, in a leather helmet with goggles resting on his forehead: Jack Larsson, the elusive adventurer everyone knows about, but no one really *knows*. We had met a few times at social events, and I had always found him fetching. But we never exchanged more than polite phrases, never been alone–just the two of us–and definitely not this close. My editor has tried to get an interview with him for years. Mr. Adventurer finally caved in, on one condition: that I would tag along on this specific journey. Why he chose me is one thing I haven't figured out yet, but here I am on an airship going straight to heaven knows where and airsick as the landlubber I am. I really hate my boss' guts at the moment.

But that's for later, I think as I look into Jack's gray eyes. Up this close, I notice small patches of green and gold closest to the pupil. Something in his gaze shifts and suddenly I'm very aware of his warm hand where it rests on my waist. I swallow and realize I have my hand on his chest, with only the coarse linen fabric of his shirt in-between. Picking up the scent of sandalwood, I tilt my head, forgetting that my own odor's far from pleasant. Jack abruptly lets go of me as if he's burned and walks away a few steps before stopping.

"Come to the captain's cabin when you feel better," he says over his shoulder. "I have something to show you."

"How can you be captain when you don't have a crew?" I call after him.

He doesn't bother to answer. The tails of his long leather coat flap in the wind as he walks away. I slump against the mast and take a few deep breaths to steady myself. From where I stand, the ground below us isn't visible, only the blue skies and a few clouds forming on the horizon. The tight ropes securing the air-balloons and sails vibrate in the wind gusts. I nearly topple over when a puff of steam hisses and the mast moves to adjust its angle to the wind, with the sails automatically trimming themselves. I cross the deck falteringly, doing my best to adapt to the ship's heaving. The contrast to the large dirigible that took me to the meeting point couldn't be greater. This two-masted airship–red with a round belly as if something's hidden in it–is remarkably fast. Something I unfortunately noticed while hanging over the railing.

I pause wearily outside the cabin, trying to pull myself together, but I desperately long to sit down and rest. Most of all, I want to go down to my quarters to wash and change. A discreet sniff tells me that would be a good idea. *Well, that has to wait,* I think as I enter the captain's cabin. *Let's hear what he has to say.*

Jack sits with his feet up on a large table full of instruments, maps and a giant teapot. He casually rocks the wooden chair while studying what looks like an airchart, absent-mindedly playing with a pencil. Without taking his eyes off the chart, he points at a chair at the other end of the table.

"Sit down. Help yourself to some tea, if there is anything left in the pot. There are biscuits, too. You'll feel better after eating something. Just gonna check the course, then I'm yours." He quickly looks up. "To show you what this journey is about, I mean."

I reach for the table and sit down, grateful for the distance. The teapot's less than half full and when I pour it, the aroma of peppermint spreads with the steam. I take a biscuit and gently bite off a corner. It tastes like paper and crumbles in my hand. A quick glance at Jack assures me he's busy, so I leave the remains on a napkin and feel content sipping my tea.

Just in time for my second cup, Jack abruptly stands up and his chair falls back with a clatter. He places the airchart in front of me and pours himself a cup.

"Look here," he says, pointing with his pen at a spot drawn on the map. I stand up to get a better view. "This is the location of Oninho Sarang, an island nation that perished several hundred years ago. No one knows why and it's been a mystery exactly where this kingdom was located."

"Until now?" I take a sip of tea and peek at him over the rim of the cup.

"Until now," he repeats and meets my gaze. The tea ends up in the wrong pipe and I cough, but wave at him to continue. "As we speak, we're closing in on the island. With this speed, we should be there in four days. Or sooner."

He picks up a biscuit and takes a bite without the rest crumbling to dust. "But to start from the beginning. A few years ago, Sir Robert Bratt, the well-known explorer, died in a very tragic riding accident. I'm sure you remember the headlines in the press, there were columns written about him for months."

"I do remember!" I say. "I went to several of his lectures, they were fascinating."

"Yes, I noticed you a few times." Jack pauses and clears his throat before he continues. "When they went through his estate, they found three identical golden metal eggs that Sir Robert believed came from this island."

He points at the airchart with the biscuit and crumbs fall all over. "The rumor was that each egg contained a map leading to the Oninho people's national treasure. Exactly what that treasure consists of, no one knows. Bratt's notes on the subject are very sparse, or should I say, difficult to interpret."

The last piece of the biscuit goes into his mouth and he chews thoughtfully. A crumb is stuck in the corner of his mouth. Fascinated, I can't take my eyes from it where it sits between the smooth cheek and the arched landscape of his lips. Unaware of my gaze, he slowly licks it away. I firmly put the teacup back on the saucer. Jack looks up at the sound and I quickly close my mouth and force my brain cells back into order.

"What more do you know about Sir Robert's notes?" I ask and sit down again. "How do you know that the island is right there? And where are these eggs?" I add, but I have a pretty good suspicion where Jack's going with this.

"One was destroyed in a fire not long after Sir Robert died. Wasn't an accident, though, if you ask me. These eggs are coveted among certain groups of people, so don't count on us being the only ones going after the treasure."

I can't help but to look through the open doors at the still blue evening sky. "What, you mean we could be followed?"

"That's something you have to be prepared for working in my line of business, among a lot of other things. News of a breakthrough travels fast."

"You've had a breakthrough, then?" I turn to look at him.

Jack flashes that wry grin of his. "I have." I can't help but to smile back, glad I'm already sitting down.

He opens a plain velvet bag and pulls out a decorated golden egg, slightly larger than the palm of his hand. I can't take my eyes off the masterpiece.

"Sir Robert's notes mostly contain legends that belong to the island," he continues. "They tell of a people who worship *Kesuakuh*, a bird god with power over life and death, from the cradle to the grave and after. Others talk about the 'dome of death' in the heart of an inaccessible area, several miles from any villages, saying it's conjured by some form of evil magic, and that there's a point where all paths abruptly end. Nobody knows what's beyond that point." He looks at me with sparkling eyes.

"But we'll be the first to find out what it looks like?" I ask skeptically. "And then what, find the treasure and live happily ever after?"

"Yes, exactly that." He laughs.

"And the third egg?" I look at Jack as he falls silent, confused. "You said there were three of them," I say to clarify. "Where's the third?"

Jack makes a face that I fail to interpret, but it disappears in an instant. "It's in the hands of the biggest jerk on this planet," he says, handing over the egg to me. "Not someone I like to talk about, though."

I frown as I accept the egg cautiously, once again extremely grateful that I'm sitting down. The gilded shell is covered by a fine filigree grid, except at the top where it's completely smooth and polished. A flower vine divides the egg into four quarters. In two of them there's nothing but the grid, but in the remaining two there are small figurines, one in each. I stoop to get a better view.

"Are those torches?" I gently caress the one to the left with my thumb. The base of the small figure is more in relief than the rest, which looks like a funnel with folded edges and a conical pillar protruding from the middle.

"It's a flower, *Miquiz calaohuayan*," Jack replies. "Translated, it would mean *'verge of death'*. I call them death flowers."

I wrinkle my nose. *How awful.* Just then, the ship heels in a squall. Cups and books slide to the other side of the table and I almost fall off the chair. My thumb slips over the base of the flower as I try to regain balance. A faint clicking sound makes me stare, first at the smooth surface of the egg and then at Jack. *What have I done?*

"How did the grid disappear?" I glance at Jack. "How do I get it back?" I press the base of the flower. Nothing happens. I try to push it down and to the left and right. Nothing.

"It doesn't seem to–" I say while pushing the flower upwards. The grid snaps in place with a distinct click, becoming visible again.

"Oh!" I say and turn to Jack. "Did you see that?"

Jack laughs. "Well done, you're fast. That took me several weeks to figure out." He takes the egg and shows me how to open it by pushing both death flowers in opposite directions at the same time. A gap appears in the narrow flower vine that divides the egg into quarters and the front opens up like doors.

I gasp. An exquisite, golden, mechanical bird spreads its wings and sings in a lifelike way. Its head moves from side to side while the beak opens and closes at regular intervals. Under the twig the bird is sitting on is a small nest with five minuscule eggs in bright colors.

"You see these?" Jack stands next to me and points at the open egg. Lines form an intricate pattern around the entire inside. "It turns out that these aren't just random lines, but a map of how to get to the island."

He reaches past me to grab the airchart lying on the table. He holds it in front of me while he describes how he managed to find the right part of the coast. I glance at his mouth as he speaks, my eyes getting caught on his lower lip. It's not until he starts leaning in that I notice he's stopped talking. A part of me wants to meet those soft lips, feel them touch mine, but the small shard of reason that's still at work in my brain makes me back off. He straightens up quickly and picks up the egg, closes it with a click.

"I have provided you with more practical clothes," he says with his back to me. "They're in your cabin. I hope they'll fit."

"Thank you." I stand up, happy to have a reason to leave, just as much as looking forward to changing out of my creased and stale traveling outfit.

. . .

The days rush by as fast as the wind, and I find myself enjoying the company. Jack has so many stories to tell, and yesterday at dinner I couldn't stop laughing after he told me a really crazy anecdote involving… no, I can't even think about it without cracking up again. I tighten the belt of the wide trousers, tuck the shirt collar under the coat of coarse, navy-blue cotton and roll up the long sleeves before going up on deck.

I cautiously walk towards the railing but stop at a safe distance. There is nothing but clear blue sky around the ship. *Or, what's that?* I squint to get a better view.

"Jack! We've got company!"

White sails are visible in the far distance. Jack comes running but stops abruptly when he sees the other ship. He pulls down his goggles and lowers a thick lens to his left eye. I find I can't breathe. Jack swears loudly as he snaps the lens close.

"Who is it?" I ask, daring to take a few steps closer to the ship's side.

"The one who has the third egg," he says through clenched teeth. "Damn you, Burt!" He walks up to the railing and looks ahead for a long time before walking straight by me on the way back to the captain's cabin. I follow, at first silently watching as he throws a few things in a bag and finally places the egg on top. He looks worried, not at all the confident person from when I came aboard. Finally, all my questions come at once.

"Who are they? Are they dangerous? Do they know as much as you do? How fast can they catch up? Can we go faster? Is there anything-"

"Can you be quiet and let me think?" he snaps.

I rest on the doorframe and cross my arms over my chest. "I thought you wanted a journalist on board asking questions?"

He straps on two modified revolvers, a giant jungle knife and shoulders his bag before stopping in front of me in the doorway. "I didn't ask for a journalist," he says, holding my gaze. "I asked for *you*."

Then the moment is gone and he takes off across the deck. "Are you coming or not? We don't have much time!" he shouts back at me.

Before I have time to answer, something hits *Prudence* hard on the side. The impact sends tremors throughout the deck, and I fall down on my knees. Jack disappears through a hatch midship as another object falls, whistling through the sky over my head, and continues down the other side of the ship.

"They're shooting at us!" I scream as I scurry down the ladder after Jack, who's pulling levers and flipping contacts on a big board. A type of vehicle I've never seen before takes up most of the space, secured by wires. It's both angular and round, with a tapered front resting on a small wheel, a narrow open cockpit and a shiny, round rear part with a big wheel and oxidized exhaust pipes.

"What *is* this?" I stroke the rounded surface, so dark red that it's almost black.

"Meet my Ant!" Jack says, turning the last knobs and handles before joining me.

"Your aunt?" Another explosion makes me jump.

He chuckles and hands me a leather helmet similar to his. "Ant. Hurry now, hop in and buckle up! And whatever you do, don't look. In any direction."

"How can you be so calm?" I whine, but I do as he says. Jack seats himself in front of me, pushing and pulling buttons and regulators. Ant coughs to a start and two metallic antennae emerge from the head to steer with. Jack checks something in a periscope and pulls two levers on the floor. A hatch opens beneath us and, simultaneously, a giant anchor falls to the ground.

"Hold on tight!" he shouts over the noisy engine. One second Ant swings slowly in the wires and the next we're free falling and the wind's rushing by. I scream and wrap my arms around Jack, but he's just laughing, high on adrenaline.

Before impact, I hear Jack push a few buttons. Thrusters help dampen the fall and we land softly in a clearing between the ocean and the jungle.

Firmly on the ground, six jointed legs extend from the middle part of the Ant where we are sitting. With my head still spinning, I look around while Jack makes the machine speed up. All is green, as far as the eye can see. The tall trees and the undergrowth look sturdy and dense. The humid and hot air makes it hard to breathe. Grabbing the sides of the wildly swaying Ant, I turn around and notice the other ship's already visible behind the anchored *Prudence*.

"They are coming!" I shout to drown out the engine roar. Jack doesn't answer, but accelerates. Ant picks up an astonishing speed as it crawls over the uneven ground and soon we are deep into the jungle, with no sign of the other ship's crew.

• • •

After an eternity in this rocking insect, Jack suddenly brakes to a halt and is off Ant before I have a chance to react. "Give me an apple from the basket behind you."

"What? Is this real-"

"Just give me the apple, dammit!" he says, without breaking eye contact with something up ahead. He throws the apple and before it reaches the highest point of the trajectory, something invisible smashes it into a mess.

I flinch. *I didn't see that one coming.*

"As I suspected," Jack says and draws his knife. "I'd bet this is the edge of the dome of death." He moves slowly forward, chops sweepingly with the knife in front of him to discover other unpleasantries before they find him. The thickets rustle; everything seems to be alive and moving. Further down where Jack's moving, I notice statues are placed at regular intervals in a row. Some are overgrown with moss and other greenery, but others... I inhale sharply.

"The statues!" I shout out to Jack. "They're just like the ones on the egg! Use them to remove the grid!" He turns around at the same time as the ground starts vibrating.

"Bring Ant here!" he shouts back and runs to the closest flower statue. "But don't look behind you!"

94

"Wait, how am I supposed to drive this thing?"

I turn around. To the far left beside us, the trees are bending and shuddering alarmingly and the undergrowth rustles when small animals scurry past. I try to focus on how to get the machine going, but the wheels and knobs stare silently at me. The jungle cracks behind me and the ground quivers. In panic, I press the first button I see and somehow the vehicle starts. I push a slider up, thankfully clearly labeled "forward". Ant jerks to a start and jiggles before I find traction mode and can go forward at a smoother pace.

Jack has reached the flower statue and is looking at the base. I notice he stiffens and then launches forward to pull on something. The cacophony of engine roars and scared animals forms a sound wall behind us that I don't feel like meeting with soon. Jack falls backwards when the lever he was pulling suddenly gives way. There's a flicker in the air in front of us.

"Give me another apple!" Jack shouts, back on his feet and running towards Ant and me. Instead of giving it to him, I hurl it myself. Nothing happens except it falls on the ground a good distance away.

Jack whistles. "Nice throw!" he shouts and jumps up on the side step and climbs in. With an experienced hand, he smoothly gains speed and steers Ant towards the heart of the dome of death.

Behind us, the roar of engines increases in strength, the vibrations in the ground transfer through Ant's legs to the cockpit. The trees and undergrowth rush past us like a green wall, until they abruptly end in an open space. Jack slows down and kills the engine. In front of us, a large square is laid out, with a smooth rock wall as a backdrop and ruins of what must have once been impressive stone buildings on each side. In the middle of the square stands a giant statue.

"The bird!" I point at the statue, not being able to say anything more elaborate with all the excitement and noise going on.

Jack rummages in his bag and takes out a bundle before dismounting Ant. I follow, and we jog up to the bird statue in the middle of the square. It's bigger than I thought, standing on a dais, surrounded by four death flowers made of stone. Outside the two main buildings—or remnants thereof—are other statues.

I barely have time to notice that the statues look royal when the roar behind us rises to a crescendo. Birds and animals flee for their lives as a bullet-shaped vehicle rolls in, trampling down half the jungle doing so. With a loud bawl, it stops and the engine shuts off.

The silence is deafening, then the metallic sound of a hatch being screwed open echoes across the square. It opens on top of the round vehicle and a head pops up. I can feel Jack tense up next to me.

"I knew it was you," says the dark haired man as he wriggles his broad shoulders up through the hatch. "Got yourself a new airship, have you? It's been a red splinter in my eye for too long now."

"I hope it sticks, Burt," Jack answers through gritted teeth.

I watch as the man jumps down to the ground. "Jack, who's this?" I ask.

"'Jack?" he says with a jarring laugh. "Is that what you call yourself these days? Well, what do you know. I'm glad your mother can't see the state of you." The laughter is gone as quick as it came.

"They call me Hawke, not Burt," he says to me with a mocking bow, which makes me decide on the spot only to call him the latter. "I'm sure you'll be told the whole story one day." He turns to Jack. "But I do thank you, my child, for all the research you left when you ran off."

He looks at the statue in the middle of the square, raises both his arms as if he owned the world. "I've found *Kesuakuh*!" he says with a condescending glance at Jack. "Another great day of victory for me!

Sorry, kid, but you're not a part of it." The loud, shrieking sound of his laughter makes me think of his namesake.

"Anyways," Burt says, back to being stern again. "You two can leave now, nice and easy." He pulls back his jacket just enough to show a revolver. "I promised your mother I'd behave if I ever met you, but I do have a few things to take care of here. Well, then. Go on!"

He waves his hands impatiently to chase us away, turns around and takes in the large bird statue before pulling out his own golden egg. Even at this distance, it's clear it hasn't been taken care of. Jack seems to have noticed it, too.

"Have you tried to make an omelet, Father? These eggs *are* hard to crack."

Burt grants Jack a grim glare. "You've always been a wisecracker with strange ideas. But it's hard-working men who bring home the treasure! And it's definitely going home with me today. You still got that notion that anything found should be in a museum?"

He laughs. "You naïve little bugger."

The man forces one side of the egg open. Jack hands over the bundle he took from his bag to me. Confused, it takes a moment for me to realize it's his egg. Our egg. *We're in this together now, right?* I'm about to pick it up when it moves, a faint but distinct vibration. I glance questioningly at Jack, who just smiles back and nods his head towards the statue and the other egg. Astonished, I pick it up and can't help but open it, at the same moment as Burt finally opens the second door of his egg. Both birds simultaneously start to sing in harmony. An almost imperceptible movement on the statue of *Kesuakuh* catches my attention. The others don't seem to notice.

"Treasures fading away in a corner of the museum do no good," Burt continues. "If I sell them, I can accomplish so much with the money. Like building new and bigger machines that can bring me greater treasures than anyone has ever seen."

"It would be nice if you went as far away as you could and stayed there, so we wouldn't have to see you again, ever," Jack mutters.

Burt spins around and glares at us. "I heard that!"

When neither of us answers, he continues with his investigation of the statue. Tense, we watch him work. I can't keep from stroking my fingers over the small bird's chest in the open egg lying in my hand. Something's vibrating in there, as if its heart was beating. I gently press my fingertip on the spot. The vibrations stop, but instead there's a buzzing sound as it starts moving. I gaze in fascination, then at the large stone statue and the rock wall behind it.

At the same moment, Burt succeeds in finding a mechanism. With a triumphant laugh, he pulls the protruding part of the right death flower to the side and the statue unfolds a wing, squeaking. On the inside, a symbol's repeated over and over.

"Ah!" exclaims Burt. "The *Xettru*! Of course, it should be a royal scepter!" He follows the direction of the wing and points. "This is how it goes, kids. A royal sign of a royal treasure. Same symbol on the wing as on the statue in front of the building over there. And what's the statue? A king, of course!"

He quickly picks up his things. Jack feints a move as if he intends to run, but Burt sets off surprisingly quick. "Sorry, squirt, you pull the shortest straw again," he shouts back at us.

Jack stands still in the sudden silence and watches him go. "I hope he'll get lost in there," he mutters as the old man disappears into the building. "At least a little." Then he starts moving.

I hurry after him to the dais. "I think I know–" we both say at the same time, grabbing the left flower at the base of the statue and pushing it to the opposite side as the other. The other wing opens but nothing more happens.

"I was so sure!" Jack sits down, head in hands. I remain in front of the statue of *Kesuakuh*. On a whim, I stand on my toes and reach up to touch the circle I noticed earlier.

"Have you seen this?" I say and pat the circle with my hand. "The small bird in the egg has a similar one." The whole statue hums and shakes when the bird slowly pulls in its wings, lowers itself, and spins around. I veer to the side to avoid being hit, and end up falling from the dais with a surprised yell.

"I've got you!" Sinewy arms catch me before I hit the cobbled square, but still we collapse in a heap. Somehow, I land on top, inches from his face. He locks my gaze and I can't breathe. With my heart beating fast, I lean in, gently pressing my lips against his. This time neither of us flinches or backs away. Instead, he places his hands on my cheeks.

"This is what I wished for when I asked for you to come with me," he whispers.

The sound of the statue coming to a halt with one last grinding thump makes us pull back from our embrace. The complete silence lasts for a few long seconds before the smooth rock wall at the end of the square moves and reveals a shrine. Above the altar, a picture of *Kesuakuh* is carved with its wings outstretched and its beak open to the side. I turn to Jack; the look in his eyes is priceless.

I stroke a strand of hair from my face. "They really loved their birdie!"

Jack laughs and pulls me to my feet. Together, we run across the square and up to the altar, where a large nest with five polished eggs in bright colors rests. Jack exhales as he reaches out to pick one up. "Look at these gems!"

I scrutinize the picture of *Kesuakuh* on the wall. It has the same circle as the others. To be able to reach it, I climb up on top of the altar.

"What are you doing?" Jack wonders as I stand on my toes and press on the round surface with my hand. With a click, a small box protrudes from the wall. I look at its contents, and then at Jack.

"Give me a couple of days to write a suitable article to send to my boss," I say, picking up the object from the box.

"And then?" he asks in a tense voice.

I hold up the small oval case into the light from the doorway, feeling along the edges for hidden hooks and mechanisms. And finally, I feel it.

With a suitable buzz, the lid divides and folds out into wings. Not a bird this time, but more like a big bee. A small head protrudes from a hidden opening. Spinning gears and springs move in steps around a round dial. But it's no ordinary watch. Instead of numbers, I find myself staring at the points of a compass rose. At the center, a needle spins and swings at its very own pace. I smile.

"Then we'll find out where this little fellow's taking us."

* * *

EMMA BERGLUND is a writer living in Sweden. Emma writes any story that comes into her head and has published works with Fåglar Förlag (Sweden) and CovWords Magazine. When not writing, she likes to scamper into the woods on horseback or sit at home watching K-dramas.

cov-words.coventry.domains/volume-12/
www.faglarforlag.se/bocker/halsingesagor/ (in Swedish)

The Baron of the Moon

BRIANA BEDORE

LUNAR TWILIGHT WAS already a day old. The last dregs of sunlight scattered through the atmoshroud, dirty and darkening. It would be full-night by morning, and General Mateo knew she was out of time. During the weeks of daylight, it was easier to placate the people of Luna Terra and Pluto's delegates both, promising that the Far-side Expedition would miraculously return at any hour… but the Baron of the Moon and his team were still missing, Mateo's son among them, and the oncoming fortnight of darkness would be hell on hope.

Even so, she wasn't about to roll over for these gloomy bastards.

The two black-clad Plutonians in her office loomed like long, day-end shadows. The Solitary Empire always sent its goons as a symbolically tidal-locked pair: an administrator and a minister. These two had come to see her every day, like carrion birds circling lower and lower, expecting to collect their pound of rotten flesh.

"Surely you understand, General," the Magistrate said, leaning closer. He clenched his blunt teeth, tobacco breath straining through and spilling all over Mateo's desk. "Your services as Steward of

Palace Selene are no longer required. If you do not willingly step aside for a new feudal lord to be appointed, the Solitariate will deploy troops to remove you by force."

"I understand." Mateo shifted in her high-backed chair with an exaggerated, careless sigh. "I understand that the Solitariate is more than willing to send troops to capture the territory, but couldn't spare the manpower to aid in search and rescue. Curious, don't you think?" She would be out searching the Far-side herself, except that she was the last line of defense between Palace Selene and the cold, black hand of Pluto.

"It is not in the Solitariate's interest to support childish, pointless wanderings across the gravely vacuum of a lunar territory with no resources, no trade benefits, nothing but dark-age nostalgia to—"

"Now, now." The Chardinal from the Church of Charon sidled up to pat the Magistrate's shoulder, priestly robes draping around their small body like hunched wings. "Every facet of the Solitary Empire is precious to our Plutonian Empress. Even remote Luna Terra."

The Magistrate scowled and stomped away to pace, nearly toppling the little Chardinal who couldn't flutter out of his way fast enough. They collected themself, then gave Mateo a pitying smile.

"Perhaps there is a touch of providence's hand in this tragedy," they said. "You have a holy Chardinal here, and Palace Selene is already full of dignitaries from across the Solitary Empire. If we can't celebrate his expedition's return as planned, at least we can give Baron Endymion XIV a proper funeral. One worthy of his family's... distinguished history."

Mateo's hands curled into fists and her heart surged. "I will not mourn my liege, nor those who are lost with him, until I have proof of their death. Have your troops find me a body to bury and Luna Terra is yours."

The Magistrate laughed, a sharp sound, his jaw still tight. "The entire Solitary Empire is a black sea with a few pebbles of civilization churning in it," he said. "The lost are not found; no one needs bones for a funeral, they barely need an *explanation*. Here's one: the Expedition fell into a lightless crater and never crawled back out. Or more likely, fell to gross incompetence. After all, the line of Endymion has never produced anything more stunning than a string of licentious patsies. Endymion XIII, old Edd13," he pronounced 'eddy' by scrunching his nose and baring all his teeth in a disgusted sneer, "was probably the pinnacle of his noble house, and his son has compounded his legacy as the incompetent Baron of a barren moon."

"Perhaps young Endymion was—" Mateo swallowed and corrected herself, "*is* guilty of harboring the naive daydream that his fiefdom might have more to offer than resort towns with a view of old Terra. I can think of more grievous sins. Here's one: a Solitariate Magistrate slandering a feudal lord while standing in his very stronghold. You will speak of Endymion XIV with respect. Whether or not he still lives."

The Magistrate exhaled like a popped airlock, then dabbed at his forehead with a handkerchief while he tried to work up enough hot air to make a retort.

The Chardinal took the opportunity to tag in. "Your loyalty honors us all," they assured Mateo with the cloying condescension particular to religious figures and nannies. "But you *must* think of the people." They gestured out the window to the capital city of Seventeen, its marble towers dull against the soap-bubble aurora of the atmoshroud. "The Capital is a hive of rumors and fear that will fester over lunar night. The subjects need to know what will become of them. Endymion was heirless and unmarried."

"Endymion is engaged to Commander Olivier, my son," Mateo said, trying not to make it sound like a confession or a boast. The couple hadn't made the engagement public, though they'd formally asked for Mateo's blessing before they left. It was a dream scenario for her titleless military family, but what's more, Liv and Endymion had grown up loving each other. Their disappearance in the wake of that joy felt like a cruel joke. Mateo wouldn't allow it to be real.

The Chardinal tapped their fists together in prayer—the Black Moon's tidal-locked symbol of supplication—a gesture of respect, or surprise.

"That is irrelevant," the Magistrate insisted, "the betrothed is just as missing as the Baron, and what's more, they aren't married, so General Mateo's clumsy attempt to use her missing son and liege to take control of the fiefdom won't—"

Mateo rocketed to her feet, hissing as she fought to unclench her teeth. The Magistrate wilted mid-sentence.

"I care only for the future of Luna Terra," she growled, "which happens to align with my son's future. My son who is missing. My son who you insist must be presumed dead. I refuse to comply. I hold vigil for the fiefdom, for our liege, and for my son. Cross this line at your peril, sir."

The office door chimed and slid aside as Thornton, the inorganic butler, hovered into the room. "Madame Mateo," he said, dipping his bin-shaped body in a modest bow, "forgive the intrusion. We have a security alert. Someone is trying to enter Palace Selene's Palisade."

His entrance put everyone off balance. Mateo kept her composure, biting back the question she always tried to ask. *Is it them?* "Supplicants from Seventeen?"

"No, madame. Two unidentified figures wearing battered vacsleeves."

Is it them?

The Magistrate and Chardinal barely had a moment to share a wide-eyed glance before Mateo barreled out of the office, Thornton whirring in her wake.

At the palace gate, she squinted into the vacuum moat through the rippling sheen of atmoshroud, begging the silhouettes beyond to clarify, begging that question.

She would've known him by his walk alone. Her son, Liv, trudged forward, carrying another man across his shoulders. Liv's vacsleeve suit was punctured and patched. The other man's was intact, marked with the Baronial panache.

"It's them. Raise the portcullis!" Mateo screamed, already reaching for a vacsleeve of her own. The membrane of the portcullis swelled, preparing the airlock chamber, as Liv collapsed in a puff of moondust.

. . .

Selene's tasteless, opulent ballroom churned with mingling VIPs and the servants weaving between them, like a hive set to harp music. Framed in its overwrought skylight above them, the immovable sapphire of Terra melted into the deepening night sky, another neglected ornament in the gaudy palace with nothing better to do than witness the pageantry. Mateo couldn't help but relate.

This congregation of celebrities and dignitaries should have been semi-strangers all on their best behavior, but instead they'd been reduced to hateful roommates in a Jovian sitcom. After weeks thrust together waiting for Endymion's doomed expedition to produce enough proof of tragedy to let them leave, alliances, liaisons, and blood-feuds had been born and broken. The fact that the Expedition had discovered jack and/or shit on the long-neglected Far-side didn't surprise anyone; it only let them complain louder about the waste of time and advocate for longer neglect. Since the young Baron was alive, conscious, and able to receive guests, Pluto stopped sniffing at the fief like a plate of untouched food and everyone could finally attend the party they'd been invited to. There was an air of vengeful relief in their interactions, a gentle "farewell and fuck you, too" in every handshake and polite laugh.

Mateo tried not to be caught up by the gossip in the grain—the business of Solitariate feudal lords was their own, far above the scrutiny of martial servants such as herself. It would be Liv's business someday. All this facade, and all the muck beneath it.

Liv. Mateo barely caught glimpses of her son in the days since his return: he either seemed to be leaving a room just as she entered it, or locked away in privileged privacy watching over Endymion's recovery. Her son had become so distant that he might as well be lost in a Far-side crater. Mateo's visceral disappointment felt like homesickness and rejection in one.

"Attention, emissaries and eminent figures all," Thornton intoned from an upper landing, his voxbox overriding the musicians' output to carry the announcement throughout the great hall. "Allow me to present your hosts and guests of honor: the survivors of the Far-side Expedition!"

Baron Endymion XIV and Commander Olivier entered together from the grand staircase in ceremonial uniform, standing more than arm's reach apart. Liv's Lunar Guard uniform was pearlescent perfection, his posture the picture of martial ideal. Endymion might have looked almost delicate next to his broad-shouldered consort, but Mateo had never seen him so thoroughly embrace the persona of a feudal lord. A blackened coronet held his long, red-gold hair in place, his chains of office as bright as his leonine eyes. He was imposing, confident. He was trying really damn hard.

Mateo could tell by their bearing that they'd been fighting. She'd practically raised both of them, so there wasn't much the boys could hide from her, try as they might to avoid meeting her gaze. Liv's eyes were red and puffy. It must have been a bad one.

"Thank you, everyone, for holding faith for my return." Endymion descended the stairs, his black cape pouring along the marble behind him like a fountain of tar. "It's good to see old friends and new faces alike after my ordeal.

"My team may have been unsuccessful in making a discovery worthy of our distant Empress's attention, but how could any of us more exemplify the Solitariate spirit than to press into the farthest, coldest shadows of our lonely lands? We know we are alone, and still we dare, we persist, and therein we find the courage to thrive in the void."

More applause, more gracious smiles from the Baron.

"While courage lies in the unknown darkness, our strength swells from our people. We will make the Empress proud through fortification, rather than exploration, until we are hailed as the exemplary Fiefdom of the Solitary Empire."

Endymion had obviously rehearsed his little speech in front of the mirror again and again. Usually, Endymion made speeches off the cuff, from the heart, and to Mateo's ear the over-rehearsal rang of insincerity. Maybe he was simply exhausted and nervous. Or maybe Mateo was paranoid, reading too much into the behavior of boys she hardly recognized on the other side of their trauma.

Liv finally glanced her way. His grimace was so subtle it was scarcely more than a blink, a twitch of the lips. Endymion had rehearsed his speech with Liv, and there was a lie in it that sat sourly with her son. A lie he was complicit in.

Once the cheers died down and the music started again, the crowd swallowed up the pair of handsome young men, everyone taking their turn to offer them congratulations, sympathies, assertions of faith, on and on. Mateo kept them in the corner of her perception, like the cool, unwavering eye of old Mother Earth. After a time, Liv put his hand on the small of Endymion's back and leaned into the conversation to excuse himself. He slipped away and Mateo followed.

"Spare a moment for your mother, Commander?" She fell into step beside him. "You've been avoiding me since you got back."

His tired-eye smile was a shadowy thing. "Not on purpose."

"No wonder you're exhausted. Lying to me over and over again must really take a toll."

He sighed, blowing away that smile. "I need to splash water on my face. Join me if you must."

They stepped into a small washroom off of a service corridor where guests were less likely to wander in. While Liv went to the sink, Mateo locked the door, then leaned her hip on the counter.

"What happened out there?" she asked.

Liv let the tap run cold as he washed his face. "You read my debriefing," he said, leaning over the sink as the water dripped off his nose and fluttered with his breath. "Our solar batteries failed, and we were trapped in lunar night. The recyclers gave out. Atmoshroud tore. A classic worst-case-scenario cascade. The others, they wanted to come back with us..." He pressed his fingertips against his eyes. "But I did my job. I brought Endymion home."

"Bullshit." Mateo passed him a hand towel. "You expect me to believe that out of my entire team of hand-picked men and women, not a single one made it back alive?"

He toweled off, then met her eyes in the mirror. "What do you want me to tell you?"

"The truth, maybe. About anything." Mateo caught a glimpse of her own reflection—a scowling matron in flinty military regalia. She tried to soften her expression. "Are you and Endymion... alright?"

Liv chuckled coldly, inspecting his damp towel. "Priorities in line, as always." He folded the cloth neatly into smaller and smaller squares. "Don't worry, he has to marry me, I know too much. Your ambitions are intact."

He turned away as if the conversation was over, but Mateo snagged him by the shoulder. "My sole ambition is a good future for you, Liv."

"Don't act like there's an option that separates me from our liege, General." He shrugged off her hand.

"We can find another way—whatever he's forcing you to hide, you don't have to protect him out of fear—"

"I'm protecting him because I love him!" Liv wheeled around to face her. "Just like I've always done!" His hands shook as he crushed the bundled towel in his fist. "Endymion killed the others. My sweet, gentle Endymion, who only wanted to treat this black-forsaken rock like it was worth a damn." Liv pursed his lips for a moment as if he could hold back what he'd already said, then he continued, voice wavering, "You can't understand what we went through. He didn't have a choice. And now I don't either."

Endymion killed the others. Every time Mateo tried to take hold of the idea, it wriggled away from her, running like water on oiled cloth. She could see the Baron as a tiny boy, his serious expression and too-pink cheeks, always too small and too intense for his age. He couldn't kill a vent-vermin, let alone one of the Lunar Guard. But Liv was too tormented to be lying.

"The tears in your vacsleeve... did he do that?" It was unexpectedly difficult for her to speak.

Liv threw his towel into the incinerator with a saddened disgust. "No."

"Please, son, tell me what—"

"Stop." Liv put his hands on her shoulders and looked her in the eye, as if she was a stubborn child. "Leave this alone. We never should have gone to the Far-side. Don't make me go back by telling you about it," he said, pulling away. "You can't follow me there."

Mateo let him go, exhaling as the washroom door clicked shut. For a selfish moment, she wondered if she preferred the grief of losing Endymion and Liv over the heartbreak of redefining them. Endymion a killer, and Liv so haunted. Her boys would never come back, not really, and she'd have to learn to love the strange shadows that had replaced them.

When she returned to the gala, the threat-assessment part of her mind kept refocusing on Endymion like a wound in her mouth that her tongue couldn't leave alone. His distant confidence looked more like a soldier's bruised soul to her now, his keen eyes predatory. Had the deaths been a kind of cold necessity? Perhaps the awful lack of resources forced the others to give their lives to ensure the Baron's survival. Or maybe Endymion had taken responsibility for their suffering and killed them out of mercy. But if either had been the case, wouldn't Liv have told her? Until she knew what actually happened, what they were hiding, she couldn't know what Endymion was capable of.

Endymion was listening to a Saturnine Weathermancer, an old shroud-weaver who hadn't visited Selene since Edd13's day. He'd packed for a party under the old regime and had spent his entire stay dressed like an idiot. He wore heeled boots and a long leather coat patched with brightly colored fur, his white chest hairs bared to Terra and all the rest. His sheepish expression was the lone dignified accessory in the entire ensemble.

"...of course it's those shoddy Mercurial batteries that bear the blame for your tragedy, Excellency," he was saying. "Saturnine shrouds are delicate, demanding, like a work of art, or a beautiful woman, eh?" The Weathermancer waggled an elbow at the young Baron. When Endymion cocked his head, the Weathermancer cleared his throat and stumbled on. "...and, ah, like a beautiful woman ... lover-person ... hah, they'll never fail you if you take care of their needs."

Endymion kept up his frosty, pleasant expression. "And this relates to my Fiefdom's relationship with the Guilds of Saturn ... how, exactly?"

"Shrouds, Excellency. You can always count on the safest, strongest atmoshrouds in the Solitariate. The Guild Masters will personally seal each one bound for Luna Terra—"

"Please, don't trouble yourself." Endymion held up a hand. "Luna Terra will be transitioning away from atmoshrouds. We're returning to dome architecture."

The Weathermancer laughed heartily, then realized it wasn't a joke when no one laughed with him. "But ... domes are grotesquely primitive. You'll ruin the resorts' views of Terra!"

"Yes, but domes don't tear, do they?" Endymion said, reaching out to straighten the Weathermancer's ridiculous lapel. With a sudden yelp, Endymion lurched back as if he'd been burned.

Mateo's hand went to her pistol of its own accord, snapping open the holster, just as Liv stepped forward, catching Endymion and letting him hide against his chest.

"Easy," Liv murmured, inspecting the baffled and mortified Weathermancer. "It was only a bit of lint." With one arm around Endymion's shoulders, Liv picked the offending fuzz off the Saturnine shoulder. "Please excuse my liege," he said. "We still jump at every shadow."

Endymion pushed away from Liv, hissing, "We?" and stalked off without an excuse.

Mateo watched him go, heartbeat thundering in her ears as she fumbled with her holster, finally clipping it shut. Who had she been ready to shoot?

Sailing into the ensuing silence with a uniquely inorganic obliviousness, Thornton hovered forward and announced, "Dinner is served." The guests filed into the dining hall, accompanied by the reassuring susurrations of their weirded-out whispers.

The Survivors were seated at either end of the long, immaculate table. The rest of the dignitaries were placed along the spectrum of the middle, with The Most Honored Plutonian Magistrate and Chardinal seated to Endymion's immediate right and left. Mateo, a humble military officer, was stranded halfway between the Baron and her son.

Once everyone was settled, a team of footmen units placed shallow bowls of steaming, rich risotto before each guest with mechanically choreographed elegance. Real Terran rice, animal protein broth, and dairy. Absolute luxury. Endymion looked into his bowl with a bizarre, resigned horror, as if it was his third helping of human bacon, while Liv visibly gagged. Everyone wondered if they should avoid the risotto, too, but gradually the awkward music of silverware on porcelain filled the hall.

The Chardinal dove into the meal with a decidedly un-monk-ish delight. "Your Excellency," they said, cheeks bulging with food, "I can't tell you how relieved I am that you've returned to us."

"Thank you," Endymion deadpanned, smoothing a napkin across his lap.

"The Plutonian Ministry had such a long list of potential replacements, going through them was such a daunting prospect!" They chuckled amiably and took another bite.

Across from them, the Magistrate cleared his throat. "What our most Holy Chardinal means to say, your Excellency," he said, all ingratiating smiles, "is that the line of Endymion is a cherished branch of the Solitary Empire's noble tree–"

"Exactly," the Chardinal admonished, chewing, "and you traipsed off to risk your life without an heir! What were we to do? Very irresponsible." They winked as though it was all good fun.

"You were working on replacing me instead of trying to find me?"

Endymion's chest heaved. "Everything I went through. None of you cared."

The Magistrate scrambled to salvage the conversation. "Your Excellency, a fief relies upon its lord, and a decision had to be made —"

At the other end of the table, Liv coughed violently into his napkin. He hid his face and raised a hand in apology, trying to get his hacking under control.

Endymion carried on over it, temper rising, "You think that anyone could handle the Fiefdom after my fuck up of a father, but you don't know shit about what this moon actually needs—"

Liv, in the throes of a full coughing fit, crumpled into himself.

"—or anything about its void face—"

Mateo stood, whether to stop Liv's choking or Endymion's tirade she didn't know.

"—or what I'll do to protect it!"

Liv wretched, seized, and arched back. A gleaming white worm the size of a man's forearm leaped out of Liv's throat and landed in his risotto.

A stunned heartbeat passed, then the dining hall erupted.

Guests shrieked and tumbled away from the table. Mateo's mind turned to static as she unholstered her gun and half tripped over a scrambling dignitary. The worm thrashed in Liv's risotto until it managed to wriggle onto the table. Footmen units surged through the pandemonium, trying to fulfill their cleaning protocols as they toppled panicked guests.

Endymion howled, "No, no, Black Moon, no," like a fevered thing, clawing at the table. "It followed me back!" His face screwed up in an awful sob as he stared at Liv. "It followed me back wearing *you*! Not you, please!"

The Chardinal tapped their fists together over and over, mumbling horrified prayers through a mouthful of rice.

Endymion turned and pointed at them, "It's happening again, the maggots, they've taken you! They're in all of you!" He grabbed a dinner knife and jammed it into the Chardinal's gut again and again. Half-chewed risotto spewed from their mouth as they fell to the floor with the sobbing Baron.

"What in the black-skied *fuck*–" Mateo said, unable to look away, unable to take in what she saw.

"Endymion!" Liv wept between gasps, "Stop!" He dropped his napkin and a handful of fat maggots spilled out of it while another struggled free from his nostril. Liv lurched, trying to cross the dining hall. The fool was more worried about his homicidal fiancé than the fact that he was leaking worms.

Mateo called out to Liv, but her voice was swallowed up by Thornton's calm baritone instructions for all guests to evacuate even as the hall emptied. She had to keep Liv from reaching Endymion. She could deal with whatever came next after she saved her son from getting stabbed. Climbing onto the table, breaking crystal glasses and spilling that damn risotto, Mateo moved to tackle her son when something latched onto her neck. That first, massive worm flailed against her, little teeth grinding; she thought of Liv's punctured vacsleeve. She slipped in the broken dishes and fought to get a grip on the wriggling abomination.

Endymion wailed, "Give him back to me, you monster!"

Getting hold of the worm's body, Mateo pulled it taut and pressed the barrel of her pistol into the fleshy thing, "How fucking dare you touch my son," she spat, and fired. The sharp crackle of the point blank energy weapon deafened and dazzled her, but the worm fell to the tablecloth in two-ish charred segments.

Liv was talking, pleading. Mateo slid off the table and righted herself. She had to save her boy. Her swimming vision settled.

The boys were standing, Endymion slumped into Liv's embrace, his bloody fist pressed to her son's belly, twisting. Olivier opened like a slit sandbag, maggots spilling everywhere. Endymion kept working the knife, as if he could dig the creatures out of Liv, "I won't let you have him!"

Mateo had the Baron in her sights before Liv fell, clearing her shot. She pulled the trigger and punched a hole through Endymion's chest. He dropped, confused, crying out for Liv as he died.

She'd shot Endymion. Did it without thinking. Her pistol clattered to the ground. The line of Endymion, the fiefdom, the future she'd been so desperate to protect… they were all gone.

Liv curled around his wounds like an animal, pressing his hands into them as if he could push the blood and worms back inside. Mateo dropped to her knees beside her son and gathered him into her arms as best she could. Every opening in his gut seethed, and his swollen eyes twitched as the tiniest of the squirming things burrowed back into his tear ducts.

"Oh, my Olivier," she whispered, reaching out to pluck one of them out of his eye, crushing it with her fingertips.

"I fucked it up, Mom," he said, wiping his face against her coat, leaving a tear trail of half-smashed maggots on her sleeve. "They just wanted to know what we were, where we came from. They wanted to come back with us, and I…" He gripped her collar. "I didn't mean to bring them back, but I–I had to live. I had to bring Endymion home."

"It's alright." She ran her fingers through his hair. "You did it."

"No." Liv shuddered, anguished. "I didn't. I couldn't save him, Mom." He sagged in her arms, eyes drifting shut. Maggots flowed out of him like some migratory exodus, and Mateo clutched him close, not caring as they streamed over her.

I couldn't save him.

"You raised a good man, Mateo."

Mateo looked up at the sound of Endymion's voice, calm and clear.

The dead Baron sat up. His pained, half-lidded expression of death thawed, reanimating, as worms climbed into the bullet hole in his chest. Endymion stretched his jaw, sniffled, then moved clumsily to kneel opposite her. His expression was tender, sorrowful, old.

"What a mess we made of our first contact," he said. "We're so, so sorry." He reached out to touch Liv's cheek with reverence and Mateo was too shocked to stop him.

"But there's…" she sputtered, "there's nothing out there on the Far-side, or *anywhere*, we're alone in the system, what are—"

Endymion, or the things wearing him, gave a self-deprecating chuckle. "Wild, right? We thought we were alone too, until we met your boys. Pardon this, uh, awkward method of communication." It gestured to the rapidly closing bullet hole in its chest. "We're new at all this."

Mateo pulled back, holding her son away from it. "Have you been puppeting Olivier?"

"No, no. Merely passengers. He gave us sanctuary so we'd stop blundering around with the others and freaking out Endymion. Didn't expect him to accidentally puke us up, though. Real gross experience, even for us."

She stared at it. Its attempt at levity annoyed her enough to take the edge off her disgust. Or maybe that was the shock talking. "What do you want?"

"We want to fix this. Let us help you cover this up." It looked around, as if struck by an idea, and a cluster of worms slinked towards the dead Chardinal. "Let's pretend that when you killed the big worm—ow, by the way—everyone returned to their wits, the injured got emergency care, et cetera—we'll workshop the story—and then we can continue to be Endymion. The baron is definitely dead, but there's still time to save Liv. We can give your son the future he deserves."

The Chardinal sat up, spat out a mouthful of blood and rice, and waved. "Ooh," he cooed with sudden wonder. "This one has memories of another cold moon! Think we'll get to see it?"

"What do you say, Mateo?" the Baron offered its hand. "Your boy is fading fast. Either he lives, or you let everything go."

Mateo looked down at Olivier, cradled against her chest. His long, boyish eyelashes. His blood all over her uniform. "I've already done the unforgivable," she said, looking back up at the young man she killed. She took its hand. "Will you… try not to let him find out what you are?"

The Baron of Worms nodded, smiling with a heartbroken empathy that was so complete, so gentle, it could only be inhuman. With a sigh, a current of worms poured from his mouth, flowed across their joined hands, and back into Liv's ragged gut. They tugged his wounds shut like tiny, living sutures, until her son took a rattling breath.

"Endymion?" he gasped.

"I'm right here, Liv. I'm not going anywhere."

* * *

BRIANA BEDORE is an American mutt who has been sighted skulking about the Wasatch Mountains. She writes science-fantasy and fantastical sci-fi--whatever the lovely middle of that venn diagram likes to be called these days. When coaxed into polite society, she also works as a costume designer and artist's model, but is happiest pointing at pretty things in nature and going "Ah!".

Catch rare glimpses of this beast at www.twitter.com/bri_bedore.

<u>Marbles</u>

A. RAVEN DEMORY

THERE WAS A soft click. The house erupted into static and I sat awake.

Grandpa hummed to himself in the hidden room beside mine, the knobs of his radio squeaking through the wall. First one, then the other, then the antenna. I could almost see his fingers, pruny and spotted, searching delicately for each frequency. His breath counted down numbers and decimals between cigarette drags, and when he growled into his microphone, an invisible world responded.

Daylight streamed in my room's one window, which overlooked the porch. Outside, past the glass and the spider who's lived here as long as I have, I could see it was a clear day. Sand and sky rippling as far as the horizon, split by the gravel driveway that meanders to the road that goes straight to town.

I came from up that road—longer ago than I can remember—but I've never been down it again. If I think hard enough I can picture it: the midnight escape in Grandpa's truck. I can still hear his reassurance while I stared out at the moon dipping behind the mesas.

The static shifted. Grandpa calls it modulating frequencies. He must have tried a hundred of them, eavesdropping on who-knows-how-many people in who-knows-how-many languages. He'd talk about them to himself: towers and satellites, mind-control beacons and spy drones. All gibberish to me, but who am I to know what Grandpa can and can't understand?

I dressed in white in the pink morning-light, with long sleeves to hide my wrists. I put my marbles in my pocket and went to the kitchen, counting them through the fabric: three, four, five.

I heard Grandpa's radio stop on a news-man. He sat silently as the man talked about outer space while I poured cereal from a crumpled box. I wondered to myself why people would want to go there. Grandpa always said it was cold and dark, and the beacons and drones flew unimpeded, free to scan your brain and your thoughts and your immortal soul. That aside, I figured it must be to look for something they can't find here. The news-man changed with the frequency; Grandpa doesn't like talking about outer space.

I ate breakfast listening to the porch swing creak, tracing mazes on the cereal box. The radio dial halted on another song. It changed before I could pick out the tune. Grandpa cussed. My parents told me not to talk like Grandpa, but I guess he's older so he can do whatever the hell he wants. It's hard to not say things sometimes when you've been around someone like him for as long as I have.

The weatherman came on and Grandpa stopped long enough to hear the forecast. Sun, no clouds, and the optimism to suggest that there'd be rain coming soon. But I knew he was lying like always. I've never seen it rain—not here, not with my parents, not anywhere.

The beacons must've got him. Grandpa says they make you lie.

My bowl was empty and I set it on the porch rail by the unmoving spider. There wasn't any wind this morning. The sky was my favorite shade of pink and Grandpa's garden was blooming, the only green as far as you could see. Daisies and lilies all white-and-yellow, and bushes with leaves like seven-pointed crowns, all off-limits in the garden around back. Careful that he wouldn't see me, I picked a flower—bluer than the sky at noon—and hid it in my pocket with the marbles. I crushed it just to spite him. A marble rolled out, along the floor and slipped between the boards. I cursed again: some of the words Grandpa taught me, and some I picked up from his radio.

I checked again. He didn't see me. He was still turning the dials.

There was a trail of dust in the air, the faintest far-off scent of exhaust and gravel halfway up our lane. Not many people came up our lane nowadays, and I guess that's alright. Grandpa scares them away anyway.

The radio stopped suddenly on static and I heard his chair slide back with a groan across the floorboards. I heard him grumble and shrug on his flannel shirt, never buttoning it to show off his ancient tattoos. He grabbed his gun and put two shells in, then pocketed a handful more.

My heart flew. I hid under the porch the same second the front door came shrieking open. The screen slammed the clapboard siding and I heard him talking to himself. In his room, the radio drifted lazily between frequencies, and I figured he'd be back soon enough once he fired his warning shots.

I could see it now from under the porch—the marble I'd lost! Bright blue with pearly green mixed in. I put it in my pocket with the flower and the other marbles.

Now they're all together, I thought to myself.

I saw the dusty trail come closer, too, and the thing that made it. Looked like a police car. There might have even been others behind it but I couldn't tell with the dust. I squinted; yes, others. Maybe two of them. Lights, but no sirens.

Then the radio made a noise I hadn't heard before: it was the voice of a woman, but she wasn't singing. I couldn't understand what she was saying, really. Then she stopped talking and I wondered what it was all about.

The radio static hummed inside and I crawled, quiet as a sigh toward the basement window. Grandpa likes it locked, but when he's not looking I let it hang open. I slid inside, then wiped the dirt off my legs. My white clothes were ruined, but that's old news.

I crept my way through the basement past all my parents' things and the musty old boxes they left. Blankets, golf clubs, photos and diplomas, and shoe boxes full of dusty cash, tightly rolled. Grandpa's tool bench sat under a pile of dusty motors and coils. I don't ask him what any of it does anymore. He doesn't want me to know, and that's ok.

I snuck up the stairs, avoiding the fourth and seventh stairs because those are the ones that squeak. Crawling on all fours, I made my way into the radio room. I could hear Grandpa shouting from the porch. Cussing, too—real loud. Three cars, black and white, pulled in close, past a dead oak tree. A cold breeze rattled through its branches while a drone buzzed overhead. The backhoe Grandpa kept behind the house creaked.

In his room, I climbed up onto his big stool and stared the radio in the face. The knobs are eyes, and the dial's its mouth. The mouth needle shook, pointing past the highest number. The woman spoke again and the shock of it almost knocked me off the seat.

I twisted the knob like Grandpa always did, first to the left, then to the right. Cussed for good measure, frantically jiggling the knobs to get the voice back. Hit it square in the top with the back of my fist, like Grandpa does when the signal fades. The woman started to talk, slow and steady, and a man answered her.

I heard a gunshot, but not over the radio. Guess Grandpa doesn't like those people coming up the road. I picked up the microphone, playing with the twisty cord with my other hand.

The man talked, slower and steadier, one word at a time, but I couldn't understand him. I twisted the other dial to make it clearer. Cussed again for luck.

There was a loud rumble through the radio—almost as loud as the gunshot. Definitely louder than Grandpa's yelling, and I bolted into the closet, afraid he'd come in and see me on his radio. The voices continued their slow-and-steady talk, unaware of me and Grandpa and the people up the road.

A handful of bullets clattered on the floor, but all I could hear after that was him yelling at the people who'd come up the road. Lots of stern words. Threats. I could hear him loading the gun again. I felt a tear but didn't dare make a whimper.

The voice on the radio came back again, this time happy. She laughed, and I could almost envision her, a smile through joyous tears. I tiptoed out of the closet.

Then something happened outside. I saw it, silhouetted black on the bedroom wall, the people who'd come up the lane reaching for Grandpa's gun, then Grandpa shooting it, one-two, into their heads. I covered my eyes and tried my best not to scream. Grandpa's gun clicked twice. Three-four, then silence.

The woman on the radio screamed. In the silence, in the ear-ringing, dull-eyed quiet I heard her voice disappear into static. She was crying, then, and I cried for her, too; I didn't need to know what language she was speaking to know she was in pain. Was that fire in the background, half-hidden through static … or wind?

Click-click, Grandpa loaded his gun and I ran away, throwing open the curtains and jumping through the radio-room window out onto the backyard, then into the desert. As I darted away, the woman's cry was drowned out by another bang over the radio—or was that

Grandpa's gun?

Five-six. Grandpa stomped down the front porch stairs with the creak of old wood and screech of tires. The radio was louder then, the woman's tears eclipsed by groaning metal and roaring fire.

The radio cut to static and I heard another shot over the ringing in my ears and my breath cutting through my gritted teeth. Grandpa cussed at the top of his lungs—and maybe he was crying too, I couldn't tell. By now I didn't know what I was running from.

Then I looked up and something caught my eye. It was another trail of dust and smoke, but this one came from above me. It was a long, thin plume of sooty smoke that traced its way across the sky like a cloud in the place of clouds. With a flash of light it streaked from up above, then hit the desert out behind the house, under one of those big red mesas. Over in the sand flats there was a fire that was as bright as the sun. Black smoke billowed like a monster from a feverish nightmare.

I ran toward it, tracing the smoke trail with my fingers. Ears still ringing, I could hear an explosion as junk flew in every direction. Metal, glass—even something that looked like airplane wings. Smoke and chemicals stung my lungs, and in the wreckage I saw a woman in white looking away from me, toward the flames, framed on both sides by ash and twisted metal.

She was wearing a padded suit, filthy and white like my clothes. In one hand she held a funny-looking helmet with a mirrored visor, while the other hand combed her long, blonde hair that went almost down to her waist. Was that a rainbow behind her, or the glory of heaven?

I called out to her, tears streaming down my cheeks, though I didn't know why. I couldn't hear my own voice over the roar and the crackle of the fire.

She turned to face me, and her face was like a nightmare.

Marbles

It was like one of those horned animal skulls you find out in the desert: bleached white with bits of dry meat clinging to it. And were those horns? A pair of black, empty eyes looked back at me and for a moment all I could see was light of every color at once.

Paralyzed, I stumbled back as she walked toward me–slow and steady like the words on the radio–an impossible phantom with a heart of cloth and bones. The man spoke now, steady, from a box on her helmet, with the cadence of a funeral. I crawled on my back, and she just stared with those empty eyes, like she was studying me. I felt a strange comfort in them.

I closed my eyes, feeling for the marbles in my pocket, for the blue flower crushed up with them, and I remembered my family. I imagined their faces and for a moment I wasn't as scared. When I opened my eyes, she was holding out her hand. A little bolder, I stood to face her. I held out mine, too. Her gloved hand placed a little something in mine. Cold. Hard.

It was a blue marble. Wiping back tears, I thanked her, though I don't know why I was so moved by it … I hope she understood me when I said it.

"Ad astra, per aspera," she said to me in a voice as empty as space, and I wondered what she meant by it.

A rough road leads to the stars.

She slumped forward and crumpled in front of me in a shower of blood that hit me straight on. I turned around to see Grandpa, gun leveled at where the woman had stood, pale as a ghost.

"Come back here," he told me. He was weeping. "I'm sorry! I'm sorry! I ain't never gonna hurt you no more. Get the hell over here, kid. Get away from that thing. I'm so sorry I done this to you."

I heard a prayer on his breath as he approached.

My heartbeat exploding inside me, I put the woman's marble in my pocket with the rest. Grandpa put his hand on my shoulder and we walked back to the house. I turned and looked back at the woman, and for a moment I thought I saw her standing, but it was just my imagination.

Later on, Grandpa took his backhoe and dug a hole, then heaped the policemen into it along with the woman from the mesa. Towed the police cars out into the wreckage and torched them through a diatribe about the drones. Said he had to so no one would come asking questions-that it was the last we'd see of the Cydonia Police Department. And when he wasn't looking, I stared down into the grave at the woman from the radio—stared right into those black eyes of hers and tossed the blue flower in, just to spite Grandpa. I kept the blue marble she gave me, and it sat warm in my pockets with the rest of them.

The men on the news never said a word about her, and I figure they never will. All I know is that today they shot that woman into space, and she must have found something they didn't want to find. Sooner or later, more people will come, but I have a feeling Grandpa won't be able to stay here forever. I hope they try again soon, but all I can do now is hope.

* * *

Florida-based synthwave author a. RAVEN DEMORY specializes in fiction that dwells in liminal spaces, dabbling in the surreal and psychedelic. When she isn't writing, you can find her either tinkering with fast cars or composing and recording music under the nickname varinesse.

www.bandcamp.com/varinesse
Twitter @varinesse

<u>Oort</u>

S.A. SACKINGER

BEN PICKED UP his box of belongings and left the Lunar Institute of Space Exploration. *I did what I designed the company for. We found alien presence in the solar system. I just never expected they'd boot the head of the company that found it. Of course, they didn't believe me when it was I who found the alien craft out in the Oort Cloud.*

My severance package added to the billions I made with the company means I don't need them anymore to make first contact. I and a small crew can do it without them.

· · ·

"Alexia," Ben Rellik spoke quietly into his suit's mic, knowing that any louder and it would distort. As Yoshi and he left Luna City airlock and crossed the gray dust of the moon, a tall woman of African ancestry looked up from where she was driving an old battered lunar loader. "Come meet our newest crew!"

Alexia, as tall and dark as Yoshi was small and fair, put out her hand to the woman and said, "Hi. Alexia Moon: Engineer. I can also second at navigation."

"Yoshi Nagiri," the woman smiled back.

Ben grinned. "Let's head out to the ship. I'd like to talk specifics and we want to keep this trip hush-hush." He pointed to a large landing module segmented into two sections. The first one was massive, cylindrical, and standing on its end. The second one was smaller and in the shape of a wheel, with spindly spokes that extended the living and command modules out beyond the cylinder of the farming and storage section.

Once in the ship, Ben slid into a chair and spoke unceremoniously, "I want to make sure I understand why each of you wants to come along. Alexia, let's start with you."

"You know why I'm doing this, Uncle Ben. You've been teaching me about astronomy since I was old enough to sit on your lap. That's why I became a ship engineer. That's why I chose to work on the moon ... and it's why I choose to join this expedition." Both Alexia and Ben looked at Yoshi.

"Come on, Ben. You could spit out the answer as easily as I can." The words were harsh, but the smile on Yoshi's face was not. "My twin sister is in need of medical treatment. As a medical professional, you'd think I could get discounts enough to afford it, but...," her smile disappeared, "...it doesn't work that way. If it weren't for you, she'd be dead. I owe you."

"That's no reason to give up 40 years of your life to lock yourself in a tin can with three other people; to become what amounts to their nanny!" Ben's usually genial face wore a frown.

"Nanny! Ha! I'm not Mary Poppins and I can be just as excited as you are about this mission." Yoshi pinched the man's cheek.

Ben rubbed his cheek, grinned, and said, "The last little waif on this trip will be Ibrahim Duran. He's still down on Earth. I expect him to join us in the next day or two. A real nice guy. You'll like him."

Ben crossed to the computer consoles lining one wall of the living quarters of the ship where standard gravity would be kept up during flight. "I'm funding this operation and captaining the vessel because I was told in no uncertain terms that an alien in the Oort Cloud is fantasy. I can't budge anyone out of this nice comfortable tent city called Moon Base 1. Sure wish I could have convinced them to fund the expedition.

"I guess I should list our jobs: I'm the Captain and Pilot. Alexia, as you mentioned, you're Engineering and the two of us are Navigation. Yoshi, you are assigned Doctor and Chef." He raised a hand to forestall an outcry from Yoshi, "Someone has to feed us. You can argue with Ibrahim when he comes aboard. He fills in with everything else until we reach the Oort Cloud. There's just the four of us, so doubling up and helping are the only ways we'll survive the 20 year trip out there."

"20 years!" Alexia objected. "It'll take at least 30 to get out there!"

"You heard the destination, but not the way we'll get there. Have patience. All will become clear." Ben slapped a silly grin on his face and continued. "I found incontrovertible proof of a non-Terran life form. The Astro-group refuses to see it. Says it's an anomaly and we should write it off. Any alien life form, seeing signs of civilization, would contact us, they say."

"You found aliens?" Incredulity was in every note of Yoshi's reply.

"Assuming you're right," Alexia put in, "how do you expect to get to the Oort Cloud in 20 years?"

"We slingshot a few planets."

"Nope. That won't do it, Uncle Ben. We'd have to skim Jupiter *and* Saturn to make that work, and Saturn isn't in alignment. It's on the other side of the Sun."

"Not Saturn, Alexia, Uranus."

"And with that massive speed, where do you think you're going to slow down, Ben?" Yoshi asked.

"The Oort Cloud is almost completely marked with 'here be dragons' signs. Nobody knows what's out there! We'll dump our speed in the Oort Cloud. The distance from Neptune to the Cloud is enormous. If we want to survive to tell our story back home, we have to spot something we can use for a slow-down out there. Several somethings, I hope." Ben stopped as he saw the horror in the eyes of his crew. He sighed, "Ok, if we haven't found a good slow-down by the time we reach Uranus, we'll use the last two planets to slow us enough to brake to a stop. Deal?"

Both women looked at him with skepticism.

"Deal?"

Alexia slowly leaned back in her seat, shaking her head at Ben's figment. "Ben, I've known you long enough to take your word for the value of this trip on your 'incontrovertible proof' argument, but what would make *you* give up your life for this?" She narrowed her eyes and peered at her uncle. "What *is* the incontrovertible proof, Ben?"

"A dwarf planet moved."

"That's it?" Alexia raised an eyebrow.

In answer, Ben turned on the computer screen and replayed what he had recorded that fateful day.

The planet was in one frame and gone the next. "I found it again two weeks later, almost an AU away. We don't have the technology to accelerate that fast and it certainly wasn't natural. Ladies, we have ourselves an alien ship."

"Well, why are we sitting around here?! We have work to do." Alexia leapt to her feet and hurried toward the lunar loader.

. . .

The rest of the preparation to leave came and went in a whirlwind of activity. 20 years out—and the same amount back—was a long time and everything they needed had to come with them. Two days before liftoff they named the ship *The Porpoise*. They even managed to lift off on time. Suddenly, they found themselves in space and viewing the dwindling moon.

With one last keystroke, Ben secured the consoles and joined the rest of the group—the fourth member stretched out, his back in a rounded arc against the seat back.

"Hey Yoshi," Ibrahim commented with a grin, "are you interested in giving up chef work on this voyage? Your trip's celebratory cake was out of a box. We won't have any more boxes, you know. I wouldn't want to get a look at your 'from scratch' food if that's the best you can do for a celebration!"

"Ibrahim Duran! You take that back!" Yoshi hit him lightly on the shoulder and grinned.

"I think it's time to talk about the trip." Ben closed his eyes and pinched the bridge of his nose. It had been a grueling liftoff, and a headache throbbed behind his eyes. "You all know by now that our destination is the Oort Cloud. In order to do that in our lifetimes, I've determined we'll need to pull a tight swing around Jupiter as well as Uranus. Saturn isn't in a position to use or I'd include it as well."

He uncrossed his legs and crossed them the other way. "Our slowdown will need to be done in part in the Oort Cloud, so we'll be taking a long look at the Cloud over the next 20 years of our voyage.

"Ibrahim, how about you tell everyone why you're here."

"OK, Ben." Ibrahim cleared his throat before beginning, "My degree is in physics and I'll be useful there too, but I'm on this trip because I'm an alien specialist." He held up his hand to forestall the comments everyone had on the tip of their tongues. "That's specialist insofar as anyone who has never experienced a first contact with a real alien can be. There's a conference on alien contact that has been given every year for the last 210 years or so. It's called 'Contact: Cultures of the Imagination.' I've been attending since I was six."

"What does this conference do?" Alexia sounded interested.

"Each year a team of scientists and linguists from around the world cooperate to create a scientifically plausible alien for the conference. Once there, we try to communicate with the alien. It's a great exercise in expanding your mind to think out of the box."

"Do you think it'll help with *real* aliens?" Ben asked.

"I don't know, but apparently you do." Ibrahim gave Ben a sideways glance.

A beep just then from the main console took Ben's concentration away from the group. When he came back, he looked grim. "Moon Base has launched a ship and it's heading outsystem. I can only assume it's heading to the Cloud. It'll be newer and more powerful than *The Porpoise* is. If we want to beat them to the aliens, we'd better come up with a new flight plan."

"But we're already pushing our limit," Alexia grumbled.

Without another word, Ben started up his Tri-dee. Sitting around the cube, the other three adventurers leaned forward to see what happened. A cube of light expanded to contain the entire living room and a representation of the solar system came into view. "These are our choices. Here's where the alien ship is sitting as of 9 AM Luna Standard Time." A white glowing dot showed up on the screen an impossibly long way away from the inner planets.

Then another dot showed up just outside the orbit of Earth. "That's us, and that..." a third dot appeared next to the moon, "...that is the Moon Base ship."

"Please, everyone, join in." Ben leaned back in the chair. "Show me our best route."

Ibrahim pointed out his route, "Slingshot off from Mars. I know we didn't include it in the original plan because we wouldn't gain that much speed, but it looks like now we need that extra push to stay ahead. They can try the same, but we're still ahead of them. They'd have to make up that distance as well. I'm betting they won't be able to."

"I can improve the odds," Alexia said.

Ben was nervous about the excited glitter in Alexia's eyes. "Out with it. What nefarious plan are you hatching?"

"Nothing nasty. We just run silent. No identifier beacon either. I know, I know, it's against international law, but who's going to hit us? We're in space! By the time they figure out what we've done, we'll be well on our way to the slingshot position around Mars! We take in Mars, staying silent until they're past it and we'll be fast enough by then that they won't be able to pass us."

Ben pointed at the four planets near the line of travel, suddenly catching her excitement. "We plot the leanest planet hopping possible and hop them all. We'll depend on the Oort Cloud to slow our final approach. Remember, we have enough fuel to power to the half way and brake the rest of the way as well as mimicking that coming home. I'd want the computer to confirm, but I'm almost sure that gives us enough power for the slingshots."

Looking around the room, Ben read the faces of each person and made a decision. "Ibrahim, Alexia, get to your stations. I want both of you on this. If we're going to break the law, I want the three of us in collusion!"

With everyone in place, Ben made the call to run silent. "I hope this works," he said.

Ibrahim nodded. "I doubt they would make the effort if they didn't have some inclination about where we are."

"Where we are is dead in the water unless we can come up with another plan," Alexia responded.

"And we have no more time to change plans." Ben's comment brought frowns to the group.

"So, we keep trading boost planets until we can't anymore? The best we can expect at that point is to come in at approximately the same time. Nobody wins."

"Calm down, Yoshi. We need to think of all the cons as well as all the pros." Ben looked over from where he sat at Alexia's console. "What about you, Alexia? Do you have a pet theory for this? What way do you think we ought to take?"

Alexia looked down at her console screen before answering, "You can bet that Moon Base and their official crew are going to be working on new technology."

"Speaking of astronomical bodies," Ben had glanced down at the console. "I think Mars has joined the race."

Alexia got up and went to stand behind him, peeking over his shoulder. "That puts them ahead of us by a good margin. Not even an engine upgrade will put us ahead. We need something big!"

"Don't look at me for inspiration," Ben proclaimed, "I spent a year using mine to get this expedition up and going. I'm fresh out of ideas."

Silence filled the room.

After five minutes, Yoshi spoke up, "There has to be something! We're just not thinking outside the box. I'd pray, but statistics show that's impractical with something this concrete."

"How about we break for lunch and reconvene after?" Alexia's smile broke some of the tension flickering in the air. Gradually everyone got up and meandered off, waiting for the call to mess.

Ibrahim and Yoshi met in front of the food cooler door.

"I thought we had this settled," Ibrahim muttered.

"You've tried my cooking exactly once," Yoshi growled.

"Where you boiled hamburgers!" Ibrahim wrenched open the cooler door and began moving packets around.

"How else would you suggest I cook it through without burning it?"

"It's *supposed* to be pinkish on the inside."

"That's just disgusting. Nobody should eat raw meat."

"Pink is rare. Red is raw!" Ibrahim stared at Yoshi, breathing heavily. They were at an impasse and they both knew it. It took Ben coming in and asking why the cooler door was being held open for the two of them to break eye contact. Yoshi wrested the door from Ibrahim and closed it.

"Look." Yoshi ran her fingers through her hair, then gripped them in front of herself. "I think a compromise is in order. Let's both cook. We can discuss meals beforehand and learn from each other."

It was enough of a topic at the meal that no one thought to begin the discussion about travel routes until the next day.

. . .

Three weeks out from the asteroid belt Ben caught a new problem. Grimly, he pressed the alert bell. When the other three came bursting through the doorway, he asked everyone to gather round the console.

"The asteroid belt miners just broke free and are heading out to the Cloud as well!" He slumped in his chair. "That does it! We have no other way to jump ahead of them that they can't take themselves."

"The *miners* are heading out too?" Alexia asked, dumbfounded.

A groan came out of the other three. "Are you sure they could have the fuel to make it there in time?" Yoshi asked.

Ben gestured to the console's screen. "Look for yourself. See? Three others are heading back to the Moon. I'll bet good money they've pumped their spare fuel into the best ship there, along with supplies to last the whole trip."

"Those belters," Alexia grinned, "they've gotta be on a worse shoestring than we are! It should be easy to shunt them to the back."

"Don't count on it, Alexia." Ben turned his back to the screen and leaned against the console. "Those guys are crazy. They're tough as nails, too. They'll match us planet for planet."

Ibrahim kept silent, pensively crossing his arms.

"Have you nothing to say?" Yoshi asked.

"What? No. I trust in your imagination. What's there to say?"

The ship performed its duties perfectly and the speed coming out of Jupiter was sufficient to improve over the Mars ship's speed. All things being equal, they would beat the asteroid ship by a narrow margin as well.

Not so the Lunar Base ship. They too took the turn around Jupiter but their slingshot speed had been less than *The Porpoise*. The break-out point that the Lunar Base ship took showed that they were heading for a sling-shot of Uranus as well.

Ben had used that trajectory too. It all boiled down to who would gain the most advantage out of the close pass.

"By my measurements," Ben decided to bounce the calculation off from Alexia, "we should be able to gain the needed speed without any effort. We'll be passing Mars' ship in about four months. The Lunar Base ship will pass them in six months. Interesting that they didn't achieve as much additional speed as we did."

"It gives us an indication as to how deep we have to dip into Uranus' gravity well, and Neptune is now officially a slingshot planet rather than a slowing one." Ibrahim sat to the left of the main console and Ben and Alexia sat to the right of him. "I don't think we're going to have any trouble getting the lead of everyone."

Ben nodded. "Now we just need to get enough of a lead that it matters. Remember, we have to have enough time to make progress with the aliens before the rest of the stragglers come in. "Ibrahim, have you been able to study the aliens?"

"Pretty much all we know are negatives. They only came in as far as the inner Oort Cloud and no further. By now they must have seen movement in the inner planets, yet they have done nothing to contact us. Their ship is huge, but unless they plan on taking on quite a bit of material, we have nothing to account for the size. Because we have such a limited understanding of the make-up of the Cloud, we know nothing of what they could be mining."

"Why mining?" Ben asked.

"What do you mean?" Ibrahim looked confused.

"It could be anything. They could be surveying the Cloud or taking a rest or, well, almost anything."

"Huh. I just assumed, but you're right. No sense in assuming something this early on." Ibrahim scratched his cheek where stubble was struggling to survive his infrequent bouts of shaving.

"What about the ship? Besides the size, can you get anything else about it?" Alexia asked.

"Well, from the single event we have witnessed, we know that it must have some sort of inertia damping drive or they come from a high gravity world," Ibrahim answered, "and they moved to another place in the Oort Cloud that isn't very far from their first spot right before we started this trip. This makes it more likely they won't move too far away if another collection spot needs to be found."

• • •

All of the ships made the slingshot around Jupiter, gathering speed. Nobody wanted the race to last fifty years. The belters kept their same relative distance. It looked like they may not have gained as much speed as Ben's ship.

Time lagged. Although every effort was made to keep entertained, Ben soon saw a pall of depression fall over the ship's complement.

"I brought you all here because we still have several decades left of this adventure and we'll never make it this way."

"What are you up to, Ben?" Yoshi asked.

"Just thought it was about time we cross trained. If something happens to one or the other of us, we'd be hard put to replace them. So, for the next ten years, Yoshi will be teaching us medicine." Ben pushed away from the console where he'd been leaning. "Ibrahim will take over next with basic alien study. That'll cover the areas where we don't have overlap. After that we'll have a group discussion about what comes next."

"Oh, come on, Ben, I can't get a course ready overnight." Yoshi gripped the edge of the table she was sitting on. "At least give me a month to prepare! …and don't expect perfection here! I've had no classes in teaching."

"That's a good point." Ben lifted his head up and scanned the group, "Has anybody here had teacher training?"

Ibrahim sighed and lifted his hand. "I have a BA in teaching. Next you're going to tell me I'll need to teach everyone teaching techniques this month."

Ben laughed. "No, I'll give you more time than that. We'll push Yoshi back a few years and you can work up a curriculum for the next two years!"

Ibrahim groaned.

The classes worked well. Over the next fifteen years the four learned teaching, medicine, navigation, and astronomy. On lazy days and evenings, they'd get together and play a round of "Greet the Aliens". It was a solution to teaching that in itself was a bit alien.

. . .

"Morning, Ibrahim!" Alexia was always chipper in the mornings. Ibrahim was more of a night owl. They'd taken to manning stations in the off hours.

"You're up a bit early, Alexia. Problem sleeping?"

"Not exactly. I just wanted to take another look at the starboard thruster before we round Uranus." She grabbed a cup and began pouring 'coffee' into it. They hadn't packed a grinder, so the beans from the coffee plant were ground on a mortar and pestle. Taking a sip, she grimaced as always. The brew had a strong, bitter taste.

"Have you seen any possibilities?" Ibrahim asked.

"Not yet. It still looks like BR-027 is our best bet for initial slow-down. ID-001 is bigger, but it is too far away from our destination." Alexia sighed. "Can you stay on watch until I get back from EVA?"

"Sure, no problem."

Next up was Ben. He and Yoshi had hooked up about ten years back and since then hadn't made it to breakfast until now. "Where's Alexia, Ibrahim?"

"She's EVA, checking a thruster."

"Good girl! I thought that starboard thruster was acting up. It's about time she had a look at it." Ben opened the cooler and pulled out some sausages the group had made. The meat was chicken—the only animals aboard—but there were so many spices one couldn't tell. Leaf lettuce instead of bread and pickle garnish made for a strange sort of sandwich. Ben didn't seem to mind. "Oh. That reminds me. We need to put canning on the calendar sometime this month. The cucumbers are ripe and so are the tomatoes."

"So are the tomatoes what?" Yoshi came into breakfast in a robe and poured herself a cup of black coffee.

"They're ripe," Ben answered, as the chicken sausage sizzled and Alexia came in from the airlock.

"What's ripe?"

. . .

After the turn around Uranus, second in line in the race were the asteroid miners. The miners would catch up in between six months and 1.5 years. The rest of the pack had opted to begin their slow down at Neptune. Neither the moon's official ship nor Mars' ship had a chance at first place.

That meant that when *The Porpoise* looped around BR-027 there was no one there to see the mishap. As BR-027 dwarfed their ship, everyone was on hand and tense. Alexia, her hand poised to start the burn herself should the computer delay, glanced at Yoshi. The short woman had her hand poised over the engine shutoff switches. If Alexia's actions failed, then Yoshi's would be needed to prevent the trajectory from going askew. Ben flipped the switch to start the countdown. It was the main pilot board that counted. Everything started with that program.

The main engines lit exactly on time. No one could feel a great difference in speed or trajectory, but the colorful atmosphere of the giant planet pushed against the ship. Exactly on time, the attitude of the rocket changed and they were climbing out of the gravity well. The four inside the ship cheered, and Ibrahim began passing out the celebratory drinks. They were slowing down exactly as planned.

Then the alarm went off. Despite their careful planning, something was wrong. Ben, still at his console, looked down to see what was the matter and turned pale at what he saw.

It was a one in a hundred billion chance that a comet would be choosing this moment to hit the massive planet. Astronomically more unlikely than that was that Ben's ship would be entering slow-down in a slot incapable of sensing the snowball. Yet there was the comet, and there was *The Porpoise*...

"Ibrahim, Alexia, grab consoles. I need to know the precise thrust to avert this crisis, and I need it last year!" Ben had already begun plugging in an equation to get more precise numbers on the time interval they had to make the correction. He was glad the navigation class had already been covered. Having the physicist as a second navigator could make the difference between making it through with only a minor alteration in course or in careening through the Oort Cloud uncontrollably.

Within seconds, Ben made the decision to accelerate and allow the comet to pass behind them. It wasn't until it hit the planet that they realised the decision may have been the wrong one. To brake the ship, to slow down, took a braking action at a specific time; the alterations in speed happened precisely on time–just not to brake. No other time would give them as good a slow-down as the one just past.

"Ben!" Alexia shouted in her shock. "The planet was affected! We're getting a volatile reaction."

He didn't answer but immediately brought up the planetary view. A series of numbers were rushing off the screen on the right of the globe. They told a story of the atmosphere reacting to the comet's intrusion. Quickly, the gasses were roiling into space, moving into the path of *The Porpoise*.

As the ship plowed through the hot gasses, its shell began to heat up and particles breaking away from the comet pelted it. The hapless thruster that had been fixed broke off and fuel leaked from the ship. Alexia immediately left her station and leapt to the air-lock. Grabbing her suit, she began putting it on. Yoshi, seeing this, ran to help.

"We have to block that leak before the fuel is gone!" Alexia growled.

"Not until the ship cools," Ben retorted, "You go out now and it'll turn you into french fries!"

"I'll be in the airlock waiting for your bellow." Alexia wrenched open the door and hurried inside. Yoshi followed just long enough to see to the completion of locking the suit tight; then she left the airlock and began venting the air.

Once past the explosion, the ship cooled quickly. Friction from the atmosphere wasn't enough to keep the heat from leaking away into space so soon. The airlock flashed green and Alexia moved out into space, hooking her line to the bar set there for that purpose. Pulling herself along the rail, Alexia carefully transferred her line at each intersection until she stood beside the half broken thruster. She squeezed something viscous into the pipe; it froze in place. With the fuel leak stopped, Alexia took a look at the broken thruster. Frowning, she grabbed her line and pulled her way back to the lock.

Back in the ship, she put up her helmet while saying, "That thruster is dead. We need to get out the replacement. Do we have enough time?"

"Didn't you replace that thruster a while back?" Ibrahim asked.

Suddenly Alexia looked disconcerted. "You mean we don't have another?"

"I saved the old one, but you'll have to fix it before refitting."

"Let's hope I can manage it! If we break away from here at the wrong moment, we'll be adrift in space forever!" Alexia followed Ibrahim into the storage area to look for the thruster.

After about half an hour of moving ten years of history, they came across the device. It was somewhat poorer for having been stored. Together, Alexia and Ibrahim worried it around to some semblance of a working thruster; not before running shy of time. Alexia set the mended thruster in its home just ten minutes before it was needed, and hurried back inside.

Ben Rellik's hand rested steadily on the engine throttle and right thruster. "The acceleration should begin in five, four, three, two, one, now!"

His hand flexed at the same time as the console began the burn, and released when the burn should have gone away, but the thrust didn't stop then. He had to shut it off manually from the console. He realized when he did what the problem had been. While he had considered what the correct length of time would be, he didn't take into account that the ship's computation was based on the pre-emergency burn being the break-away thrust.

"Damn! The console didn't adjust the new trajectory, it corrected the record on the previous fucking burn!" Ben punched the side of the console, then shook his wounded hand. "We're going too fast and in the wrong direction by about .13 degrees!"

Yoshi went pale. "We're out of control?"

Alexia nodded, "For all intents and purposes, yes. We either head back home without stopping, or we use fuel to correct the problem and not have enough to stop in the Moon's orbit. The other option is to extend our way home to about fifty years. All of us will be over 100."

"Or dead." Yoshi's words hung in the air.

"I choose life," Ibrahim said decisively, "I choose spending my days with aliens and becoming the famous member of the first of the first contacts."

"When I get home," Alexia said quietly, "if we leave now, I'll be in my late fifties. I'll have wasted my life. I want to be part of first contact."

Ben motioned Yoshi to stop before she even started. "Yoshi, I'm sixty-seven years old. I never was going to make it home. We're going to go talk to aliens."

Yoshi's eyes grew soft and her smile sweet. "Then I do think we should be on our way."

* * *

S.A. SACKINGER is a writer living in Tacoma, WA, USA. When not writing, she likes to play D&D, and swim at the local YMCA.

cov-words.coventry.domains/volume-12/

Marriage Clause

H.L. HINKLE

GRAY. I WAS surrounded by it, engulfed in it, a tight-knit maze of cubicles spreading out across the moderate-sized room that was Acquisitions.

Robotically, my hands moved across the holographic keyboard on my desk. The latest acquisition reports. Pointless given the Company records everything we do through nano screens, but what is office work if not to pursue futility? I could be like the rest of the office and lend out my body to a mod, but I like my bodily autonomy too much. So, it's manual typing for me.

My hands slipped from the keypad as a burst of laughter broke the silence of the office. The keypad quickly clicked off, no longer registering my finger movements.

"Shit!" I said in a whisper to no one in particular.

The harsh sound of reprimand quick and shrill filled my cubicle. As a tiny rectangular piece of paper fluttered down to my desk, its red lettering telling me I'd stopped working.

"Ya. I know, you stupid machine."

It gleamed menacingly in the dim office lighting, daring me to do something about its presence. I ignored it, stretching instead.

"Buzzz…" My phone in my pocket.

My heart skipped a beat as I reached for it. Another warning ticket fluttered down in my peripheral vision. The phone message was short and sweet, but it dispelled the gloomy gray of my current situation.

"Morning, beautiful," it read with three little hearts trailing the text. Kzee *loved* emojis.

I hurried back with a reply. "Hey yourself, sexy." Making sure to dot it with at least five bright red kisses.

"We still on for tonight?" Wine emoji, nighttime emoji.

"Of course, I have the Pong booked up for the next 30 cycles." I typed, my heart fluttering as I waited for the little dancing lines to come back with his reply.

"So, what are you up to?" He knew I was at work.

"Being bored. Finishing up pointless paperwork that I'm pointlessly typing up so it can pointlessly be printed off on pointless paper to be archived never seen again."

"Acquisitions are pretty boring, I guess."

"Not really. Just the paperwork part, the actual acquisitions part can be pretty–" I paused to think of the right word. We're not allowed to talk about acquisitions. "It's not boring."

"Well, you know what's even more not boring? Space mining!" A shiver ran down my spine at the thought of deep space. "You could always come for a visit … see what life's like on the outside of the company."

My chair squeaked as I leaned back in it. It wasn't that I didn't want to see him … it was just, well … It took six months just to get there. The company would burn me if I took that much vacation time.

"You know I can't. My contract is clear, two months of vacation every cycle. It can't be rolled over or accumulated, and you're six months out."

Kzee's dots wavered as he formed his response. I knew his answer; it was always the same.

"We could just get married. That way I can see you every day, and I can guarantee that you won't be bored … at least not every day." This was followed by a slew of corny marriage emojis.

"I just think we should meet in person first, Kzee, before we take that step. What if I'm not what you want…" I bit at my bottom lip as I stared at the screen.

It wasn't that I didn't want to marry him, it was just complicated. The Pong was the only place we could be intimate, though only through avatars; it was an old, slow system that was meant simply for socializing through the far reaches of space.

I knew it sounded like a poor excuse; he had been the only person I'd ever pinged with. But the thought of giving everything up, even for him … I just wasn't ready yet.

"There's nothing about you that I won't love, Anna, but okay," his dots wavered as he thought out the rest of his reply. "The offer stands. I can wait 'til you're ready."

"Well." Part of me wavered, begging me to step into the unknown. "I should get back to work. Management is going to start charging me for the paper they're using to reprimand me."

"OK. I'll see you tonight. I bought a new avatar so it should be fun!" Smiley emoji, robot emoji.

I hit the smiley emoji in response before sliding my phone back into my pocket. Falling back into the gray despair as another warning fluttered down onto the growing pile.

We don't talk about Acquisitions

The salesman lurched forward, its limbs ragdolling around itself as its one good leg propelled it across the dirty, burnt carpet. Its blackened limbs elongated and separated from the host, but were still secured to it by the dark blue button-up and black trousers.

"Suppose I should just finish you off and call it an accident," I said, but I knew that would only get me a reprimand. Corporate wanted a sample even if it was a bloodthirsty and broken one.

"You see, this is my conundrum," I said to the thing as it bared its sharpened teeth at me. "If I provide a sample, then more of you are made. This means, I and my team are called to acquire you when you finally break and start eating your customers ... as you did here." I gestured around the room of various decaying body parts.

The thing lashed out at me, biting my ankle as I moved around it. My suit registered the attack, increasing its density so the thing couldn't pull my legs out from under me. Other than that, the overly wide, toothy mouth was nothing to my combat suit.

With a sigh, I popped its leg with a Bio bullet and watched the exposed orange-hued skin of the ankle go black. The torso seized as autotomy set in, quickly detaching itself from the leg. The host still fighting for life, as programmed.

"This used to be more fun when your brains were here," I said, pushing the barrel of my weapon into the back of its skull, its teeth still working at my ankle. The bullet sank into the flesh with a hollow thunk.

"But I guess it makes sense, in a business sense sort of way. One good or even bad torso shot, and you're just a head for months." I leaned down and wrenched the now blackened head from my ankle. "But damn, you guys were smarter back then." The torso gurgled at me, clear liquid dribbling out of the hole where the head had been.

"0053Management to 9957Anna, is your section cleared? Over."

"9957Anna to 0053Management," I said. "Package is secured. But I have to say I miss the bots … or people, why don't they use people anymore? Over." Sitting on a stack of less gore-stained papers, I watched the thing as it played dead.

The once salesman took another wet-sucking-hole breath. "God, you're disgusting," I said to it.

"0053Management to 9957Anna, too many sentient pings on inspections will do that when it comes to Bots. No one wants life in a penal for accidentally murdering an unregistered sent that can't fight back. And people have an aversion to death even if they can be rebooted." They sighed heavily over the radio. "Making gene mods the cheapest legal option. Apparently, this startup had been profitable. Unfortunately for them, the salesmen started eating the customers. The company got it for cheap. Over."

Visions of the next few years played out before me, and the dreariness it would become. The likelihood was good that these things would eventually take my position, thus shunting me into that damned gray office forever.

"You're the wave of the future," I said, waving graciously towards the torso as it slowly sucked in air.

Mindlessly, I texted Kzee, my finger hovering on the send button. I needed to take my mind off the horribly mundane future probabilities while I waited for the extraction team. I thought of his past proposal, and the possibility of an exciting unknown future. With a sudden burst of realization, I deleted the unsent text.

"Yes, I will marry you!" I typed in quickly, hitting send without a second thought.

Without waiting for his reply, I began formatting my resignation letter as the extraction team burst through the doors.

Six months is longer than you think!

The veil of synthetic silk fell back over my eyes, obscuring the bright red tag slashed across the entrance to Kzee's ship. Some of the red paint flaked off to my touch, falling between the connectors of my shuttle and the ship. The hatch door was space side, which meant someone besides us had to have been docked here recently to apply it. Cheap paint doesn't last long in space.

"Ayuh! That ship's been tagged," said the driver of the shuttle I had chartered from the nearest station. It was a pointlessly astute observation, though I don't know what else I had expected from a sentient AI. He was an old sent from the look of him, and the rickety ball of metal he called a shuttle looked even older.

"You sure you don't want to bang a yoo-ee?" he said it like I should know what he was talking about. His voice mod so thick I needed to stop and think about what he was saying.

"No!? I don't want to head back to the station." At least that's what I thought he was asking me. "I'm sure I can get it open." I let out a nervous chuckle as I worked at the release hatch's handle, sunk a few inches into the door of Kzee's ship.

I pushed the veil away from my eyes once again, as beads of sweat prickled at the edges of my hairline. I mumbled curses under my breath as I wrenched at the handle. A strange sense of unease fluttered in my chest.

What if I had come all this way for nothing? What if I couldn't get in? Nervous thoughts plagued me as I stood at the entrance of the ship. Bright red words flashed at the edge of my vision: *connection error.* My extensions were down, not helping the situation at all. At least back at the station, I could find out why my extensions weren't working. I could even call Kzee and find out what was going on.

"You can't get there from here, lady, and I don't have all day," said the shuttle driver, his voice crackling through the secondhand speakers he had taped to the wall of the shuttle.

With the screeching of cold metal, the hatch finally opened … about a foot.

"See, open!" I said, looking back at the droid. His smooth plastic face showed no emotion.

Pleased with myself, I grabbed my bags, shoving them through the small opening in the door. They clattered to the ground and skittered across the grated floor. I let out a groan; I hadn't expected grated flooring. I wiggled my toes as they pinch in the new high-heeled shoes, which had come with the dress and were unbearably uncomfortable. But this day wouldn't have felt right If I hadn't worn them. The grating was going to be a problem.

With a sigh of determination, I stepped through the crack. It was a tight fit, but I squeezed myself through, cringing inwardly as the fine fabric beadwork grated across the metal of the door. My heart sank to the sound of ripping fabric.

"Shit!"

I stumbled through, a heel catching in the grate just like I was afraid of, and with a snap, I fell to the ground. A cloud of billowing white fabric engulfed me. Digging through the white fabric, I found my broken shoe still attached to my foot … minus one heel. The door to the shuttle hissed shut, followed by a series of clicks as the undocking procedure began.

"Hey, the ship's doors are still open!" But my words went unheard.

I scrambled to the door, as images of myself being sucked out into space flashed in my mind. With a screech, the doors slid shut on their own, locking in place just as I heard the shuttle depart from the docking bay. A cold sweat blanketed my body, I slumped to the floor, my breath ragged from the near-death experience.

"I hate space."

. . .

The new, newly discarded heels made for an odd pair as they sat neatly against the gray walls of the ship. One hobbled and broken, the other still nearly pristine and filled with hope. Maybe it was an omen.

I had given in and rummaged through my luggage for my old pair of boots. Well-worn from the long journey, they were like a comforting hug after a hard day. The floor was not only grated but serrated, who the fuck does that? Maybe it's a deep space thing? I didn't know.

Unfortunately, I had found my extensions were still down. I had hoped they would link up once on Kzee's ship, but his servers seemed to be down as well. On top of that, the comms panel for the ship was unresponsive. Whatever was happening, it was happening to the whole ship. I was starting to think I should have just gone back to the station.

"Kzee!" My voice bounced off the walls, but no one called back.

Gray steel hallways twisted nonsensically as I made my way through them. The air had turned thick and hot as sweat soaked my dress. I squinted at the white lettering that lined the walls, trying to figure out where I was heading, but my eyes couldn't seem to focus. I dropped my bags as I spilled into the wall. Their glistening grayness spun around me as black dots danced in my vision. I pushed myself away from the wall, my hands coming back wet. Thin rivulets of water slowly streamed down the interior of the ship from condensation that shouldn't be there. I squinted at them, trying to focus my eyes.

"Well, that's probably bad," I said as my stomach lurched and the floor jerked out from under me. The world going black.

I should have worn black

The smell of burnt dust and iron filled my nostrils as the world swam back into focus. My eyes fought to stay closed, and my head swam with pain. The serrated grates pushed into my exposed flesh, leaving red welts as I struggled up from the ground. My feet screamed in protest, and I looked down to find my feet bare. Someone had taken my boots! My once white dress was now gray and dingy.

I turned slowly, trying to get my bearings. I was no longer in the hallway but in an extremely dirty room. It was cavernous, with small piles of metal, bits of plastic, and loose wires laid out in heaps. A dim red glow washed over it all from atop a bulky door that stood just behind me.

I hobbled over to the door, cursing whoever had taken my shoes. The door was solid, and the panel next to it beeped back at me as I poked at its buttons, but nothing happened. In the dim glow of the red light, I looked around for something I could use as a weapon. Someone had brought me there and I doubted it was Kzee. A carbon fiber tube jutted out from a nearby pile, catching my attention. Pulling it free, I found it had been hastily hacked from something, leaving a sharpened point at one end.

It was longer than I would like, but the weight was good. As I moved it around, getting used to its clunky-ness, I noticed the hatch door I had used to enter Kzee's ship earlier. It sat askew, detached from the ship, propped up against a pile next to the wall. The red tag had nearly peeled away completely from its surface. I wondered how long I had been in this room unconscious. From the looks of it, it had been some time.

The red light suddenly turned green, and the massive door behind me hissed as it began to move. Hurrying to its side, I pressed myself flat against the wall and watched light spill in from the other side. Three elongated shadows leered in through the open door.

Gripping the pole pointy side out, I silently danced from foot to foot as the floor dug into my feet. I frowned, trying to concentrate as the first man stepped through the door. With a scream, I pushed from the floor, lunging at the man. The pipe sliced through his neck as I tumbled into him. The other men screamed as I stood wincing, pulling the pole from the man's neck. Blood spurting across my already soiled dress. Of the two men left, one fell to the floor whimpering in a language I didn't understand while the other tried to make a run for it. But there was nowhere for him to go; the massive door opening only to the control room of this ship. With a thunk, his body dropped to the ground as my makeshift weapon lanced his head.

"Ha. Well…," I said, turning to the last man, intent on asking him what was going on.

He had backed himself into a corner, sobbing incoherently to himself. I opened my mouth, hoping to get some answers, but then my eyes landed on the dangling pair of boots, my boots hanging from his belt. My body went numb as the pain in my feet intensified. I marched over to the speared man and yanked the pole from his head.

"Who the fuck steals someone's shoes!?"

Marriage, it's more than love … it's a whole lot of legal BS

The man had babbled in terror, probably spilling everything. Unfortunately for him, I understood none of it without my extensions and the language mods. Though the sheer number of explosives stacked haphazardly along the back wall of the control room could mean only one thing ... *pirates*.

They had brought me to another ship at some point. In its control room, on fuzzy, outdated monitors, I watched distant humanoid figures as they scurried around the outside of Kzee's ship. They ferried bits and pieces of it to other ships in the vicinity. From the looks of it, they had been stripping the ship for a while. Leaving it hanging lifeless in the void, more skeleton than ship now except for the command deck, which hadn't been touched. "Kawaii Zed" still emblazoned upon its surface.

Unfortunately, the ship I was on had been left floating a considerable distance from Kzee's ship, and I had no idea how to pilot it. At least they had brought my bags with them. I had found them stuffed between some bombs and a wall. It looked like someone had tried to break the lock but had given up, finding it too hard. Shame for them, but great for me.

The space side door of the airlock opened, and I kicked off from the ship, my stomach instantly lurching as I plummeted to my destination. I had worn my suit off and on during the trip so Kzee and I could talk. I had considered getting something more practical for mining, and less ... militaristic. But thanks to my suits' military grade software, I now knew my extensions weren't simply out, but that someone was suppressing transmissions.

My weapon, gifted to me by the company, had stayed locked up in one of the two bags the whole trip. I hadn't realized how naked I had felt without it until then. With it by my side, I gladly left behind the gore-crusted pole.

Kzee's ship, the *Kawaii Zed*, had been military classed at some point. Eternal Entity class had been the ones to start the AI revolt, leading to the eventual independence of all AI. But how Kzee had gotten ahold of one was a question I had no answers for. Had the AI sold its casing? Keeping it would have been pointless, given AI's can't kill humans … the Asimov code seemed to transcend transcending. But sentimentality makes fools of us all. Still, it seemed impractical for mining.

The busy little workers didn't seem to notice me as I floated over them. My suit propelled me steadily in the direction of the command deck. I remembered from training that military-issued ships' command decks could detach from the main body. All this meant for me was that there was an extra airlock somewhere on its surface.

The airlock was around the far side of the detached deck. It had been left open by someone and sat about an inch from the airlock door. I silently touched down on the ship's surface before it, my bags and boots bouncing off me from their loose restraints around my waist. Everything about these pirates screamed *unqualified*.

I peeked in, finding the airlock empty. I fumbled for the floating boots; I sure as hell wasn't going to leave them behind. I had shoved a detonator into the toe of one of the boots, along with a dirty sock to keep it from floating out. With the abundance of clearly homemade explosives on the other ship, I figured I'd set up a little distraction.

Gently, I removed the sock, letting it float away; it wasn't my sock. I then removed the detonator while sliding the hatch door open a bit more before thumbing the button. A flash of light blinked before disappearing. *A silent disaster.* Carefully I slipped into the open hatch.

Suited people scurried around, frantically pushing themselves against the large command deck window overlooking the carnage. My radio crackled to life as someone switched off the suppressor, my heart thumping as their screams washed over me.

They hadn't noticed me, as expected they were too worried about their people on the outside. A man clearly in charge pushed his way to the front of the window. He shouted orders over the comms, his voice was strangely calm even in the panic. My excitement ebbed as I watched them unnoticed. Not one of them had a weapon other than maybe a knife attached to their side.

I turned my comms on:

"What's going on here, and where is Kzee?" I said, leveling my gun at the man's back.

They all turned to look at me, their hands rising in surrender at the sight of my weapon pointed at them. Startled cries and half-questions filled the radio, quickly silenced by the man with a grunt.

My finger reflexively twitched, nearly pulling the trigger at the sight of the salesman before me. Not just any salesman: an original, the ones that can think for themselves.

"It's all legal." No doubt recognizing my suit, the salesman moved slowly to an adjacent panel, where a lone cracked and well-used tablet sat.

"I doubt kidnapping me is legal."

The salesmen stopped baring its flat squat teeth at me.

"Not kidnapped, just moved out of the way," he said, reaching out to the tablet. "Here, I can show you. We have paperwork … a contract with the toaster."

"Well, let's see it then," I said, keeping my weapon trained on him.

He looked at me, unsure, but tossed the tablet to me nonetheless. It floated gently towards me. Sure enough, it was a contract, and as I read it so many things clicked into place. It was a crap contract, and I wondered why Kzee would do something so drastic.

"Take what you have and leave," I said to the salesman and his people.

He looked like he wanted to protest, but one of his people grabbed him by the arm, tugging him away. He glared at me, his eyes hard and angry.

"We will renegotiate this at a further date. As Kzee's wife, I have that option according to intergalactic law."

The salesman said nothing as we continued to watch each other. I had no doubt that if he had known who I was before, I wouldn't have woken up on that ship. His people collected their things, and soon enough they were all gone, the airlock clicking shut behind them. Within seconds of them leaving, the ship powered back on. Doors hissed shut and lights flickered as they warmed from the cold.

"Okay, Kzee!" I said to the space around me. "What's going on?"

"Anna...," said Kzee, his voice worried over the ship's speakers. "I was going to tell you ... I wanted to tell you."

I took a seat in the long-forgotten captain's chair, quiet as I focused my attention on the cylindrical tube that jutted up from the center of the room.

"I knew about your job, Anna. I have known everything about you for quite some time. I searched for someone like you in hopes that you could help me ... but I never thought that I'd get someone like you. Someone I wanted to be with. I had just hoped I'd find somebody to help me get out of this contract. Though you turned out to be so much more, I planned on telling you ... I should have told you. I was just afraid you'd leave me." He fell silent, waiting for me to say something.

"People are people, and you can't defend yourself against them." I had never realized salesmen were classified as people, and the thought made my skin crawl. "I understand, Kzee." I wasn't mad at him. If I were in his shoes ... or tube, I would have done the same thing. "But why did you agree to that contract?"

"It was only supposed to be one time. One time of them harvesting my body. I needed the fast cash to purchase mining rights, but they just kept coming back. Every time I regenerated my parts, months of mining resources, they would just strip them away."

He went quiet as the room hummed with life. "No one would do anything about it. The contract didn't specify that it was a one-time thing. Marriage was the only clause to renegotiate."

I leaned back in the captain's seat and let it all sink in. I remembered the salesman that I secured for the company. Probably still alive somewhere in a tube, its parts harvested to make new mods. Simply because it was someone's property according to a piece of paper somewhere.

"Well, you did promise that I wouldn't be bored."

I pushed myself up from the captain's chair and made my way over to the cylindrical tube that was Kzee. Not really knowing how to handle this, I curled myself around him in an awkward hug.

"I do love you, Anna."

"I love you … too, Kzee, and no one is ever going to hurt you again."

He was still Kzee after all, the only person … or whatever, that I ever wanted to be with. This is the only way I have ever known him, and I find myself … okay with it all.

* * *

H.L. HINKLE (cacklingcat) is a writer living in Washington, the state (U.S). More idea-driven than genre-driven H.L. Hinkle is currently working on a shifter dog mystery on Royal Road. When not writing, H.L. Hinkle likes to watch gaming videos on YouTube, especially horror. She also enjoys going for long walks alone, so she can listen to her favorite podcast Risk.

Twitter @cacklingcat1
www.royalroad.com/profile/143305/fictions

It's Not You, It's the Anomaly

J.P. REYNOLDS

SOME THINGS I know, in no particular order:

1. It's been 6,401 days since the Anomaly—that pulsating, rainbow-colored, oil slick of a something-or-other—appeared, floating out at the edge of explored space.

2. I have been living and working on the space station—the name changes so frequently it's not worth recording—for 9,145 days.

3. It has been 56 days since the station's last hostile acquisition.

4. It has been 18 days since Elle asked for a divorce.

5. I have 12 days to get Elle back. (I read somewhere that once a partner initiates the end of a relationship, you've got 30 days to change their mind or the chances at reconciliation drop to more-or-less nil. I know, I know—*so what have you done to get her back, Desmond?*—I'm working on it.)

. . .

I clock in for the day. I don't know why the optical scan has to be so bright, but at least it only took two pupil-searing tries today. With a flick of the eyes, I engage my LiFESTREAM, that gnat-like blur hovering in my periphery, waiting to deliver the information I need with a look. Today's list hovers at the edge of my vision. I gloss over the expected tasks before pausing on the lone oddball: *Polish the central Anomaly viewport.* Again. For the third time this week.

Rik saunters in. The infuriating bounce in his step is so pronounced it feels like he's rubbing it in my face. He's a big person in all respects: colossal physique, outsized personality, extra large ability to drive me up a wall.

"Dez!" he booms. (I would like it on the record that no one calls me Dez.) "What's the good news, brother?"

"Rik," I reply. "Polishing the central viewport again."

"These new guys are obsessed with the thing," Rik chirps. "Gotta love the enthusiasm."

I grunt in reply. I hate the Anomaly. Since it appeared, every night I only dream about wandering a psychedelic version of the station. Everything is iridescent, like it's coated in a layer of swirling, shining Anomaly goo. I think there's a causal connection, but nobody believes me because I have no "evidence."

Also, it ruined my marriage.

. . .

As Rik and I enter Mess Hall B, I can see the cream-colored metalfoam table at which I had been eating alone all those years ago when a group of researchers approached in the yellow jumpsuits of the Science Initiative. Elle had caught my eye right away, striding confidently at the head of the group. I remember looking down at my own slate grey suit and trying to quell the hope stirring in my gut. People who say you should follow your gut deserve a retroactive kick in the pants.

I had already been cleaning and maintaining the station for more than a decade when Elle and the other researchers arrived to study the Anomaly up close. The years between the Anomaly's appearance and Elle's arrival had been a revolving door of mergers and acquisitions. We didn't know back then that these would be the last years of peace on the station, that the acquisitions were on the verge of outright violence.

I can't help but replay to the scene of the day we met in my head as I work.

"Do you mind if we sit here?" I remember Elle asking with great warmth.

"Uh, okay," I replied, with that patented Desmond charm.

She introduced herself and her colleagues, the words tumbling out of her mouth anxiously. "We've been here long enough to scrub the hyperspace preservation fluid out of our pores, but not long enough to come to grips with the existential dread of staring down that pulsating, colorful hole in the universe. Or whatever it ends up being."

She glanced at my jumpsuit and put together that I was part of the station's understaffed janitorial team. "If the spotlessness of the station is any indication, you are a good friend to have. Handy and thorough." She held up a beer and said, "maybe we can trade you in exchange for some advice on how to keep our sanity?"

I accepted and we clinked the necks of the bottles.

"So, how long have you been on the station?" Elle asked.

I paused, embarrassed at how long I'd been toiling away in the same position. I didn't see how I could lie about it, though, so I answered directly.

"Handy, thorough, *and* dedicated. I think we've found ourselves a keeper, guys," she said, smiling at her colleagues, most of whom stared down at their meals nervously.

"To new frontiers and new friends," she toasted. We made eye contact as we clinked our bottles a second time and my heart rate picked up like I was running a race. (Probably. That's not a thing I do.) I was a goner from the start.

With her combination of intelligence and charisma and my, well, *this*, we weren't exactly an obvious pairing, but she seemed to like me, so I went with it. I carry this gut around all day long and look where it got me.

Back in reality, I can almost convince myself that I see the outline where my empty tray sat that day. I keep scrubbing the table with a sigh, trying to wipe away the memory.

. . .

"Yo! Dez!" Rik chirps in a way that suggests it isn't the first time.

"Huh?"

"Do you want to go top off the recycler or finish the tables?" he asks.

"I'll take the tables," I reply. Rik is a pain, but sometimes I feel bad about how I treat him. Not bad enough to pay attention to his nonsense, but at least I can make it up to him by taking the worse task from time to time.

I start on the table next to a group of Station Defense Alliance agents in their olive green jumpsuits. Luckily, they remain oblivious to my existence and continue their conversation. Near invisibility is the main perk of this job.

"Have you guys gone to any of these town halls?" I hear one agent ask.

"No way, bro," says another. "I wasn't raised that way. These Emissary of the Reflection guys freak me out."

"Dude! Watch it! They're not messing around. I've been here through three acquisitions now, and those guys are *different*."

I have to agree. The previous occupants were corporations hoping to generate a new round of funding on the potential uses of the Anomaly, not religious zealots. These guys actually believe in something and it's terrifying.

"For real," starts another, "I was talking to Julia…"

"*Talking*. Is that what the kids are calling it these days?" another snickers.

"Shut up," Julia's implied paramour replies, stealing a protein cube off of his buddy's tray. "Anyway, you know she's pretty high up. She said that now that everybody has settled in, they've started calling it 'the Abomination.' She's on weapons today and swears they're going to fire on the thing."

Wait, what? I think.

"Wait, what?" I say.

The agents startle. One turns to Julia's confidant and says, "Man, I told you. You can't be talking like that where anyone can hear you."

"It's okay, I'm … not on anyone's side. I'm on the station's side. Do you know when this is going to happen?"

"I don't know anything, old man," says Julia's confidant. "I don't know what you think you heard."

I nod and glance at my LiFESTREAM before I move along to the next table. His identifying information floats in the margins of my sight. Junior Officer Sang-Kyu.

Things that pop into my head, in order:

1. Elle is out there in the research shuttle.

2. I'd rather she didn't get blown apart.

3. Are we sure the Anomaly won't retaliate in some way?

4. If I stop the attack and save Elle she has to take me back, right?

. . .

On our way to the Third North Arterial Pass, I have my LiFESTREAM search the station directory for "Julia." Filtering for SDA agents, I get 15 hits. Not bad for a station of 12,000, but still too many. As Rik prattles on (something about dreams and psychic connections; he really is hopeless) I direct my LiFESTREAM to ping all 15 Julias with the same message: "Hey–I just bumped into Sang-Kyu and he gave me something to pass along to you." I'm banking on only one of the Julias knowing Sang-Kyu. Hopefully they're in the smitten-and-passing-notes phase.

Rik is busy setting up the beacons that ping anyone headed this way, alerting them to take another route. When someone comes trodding through before the floors have dried, we have to start over. Also, I guess someone could fall. This leaves me to reminisce while I start polishing the floor.

The first living pod Elle and I shared was near the Third North Arterial Pass (or Th3 NAP, as it was being marketed back when we moved here). After yet another acquisition, they converted the researcher housing into a suite of executive lavatories and we took the opportunity to move in together.

In the years after, the acquisitions became increasingly violent. Elle and I were fighting all the time as if we were determined to outdo the acrimony of our surroundings, but I didn't understand what she thought I could do. *I keep this whole station in order so that you can do your work, what more do you want from me?* I'd think.

I even told her I'd be willing to transfer to another station, to leave the home I'd lived in and tended to for the last two-plus decades, just to get away from the fighting and that awful astral phenomenon causing it. She'd just say that I didn't understand, that I wasn't listening. Looking back, I should have seen her leaving me coming.

. . .

As Rik and I work on the Th3 NAP, I get responses from Julias 1 through 11. The general flavor is "I don't know who you are and I don't know any Sang-Kyu." The level of decorum varies.

On our way to the central Anomaly viewport, I get the response I was waiting for. Julia 12 wants to meet me before her shift in 15 minutes. She confirms that she can meet me at the viewport and a bud of hope blooms in my chest. *This is it,* I think, *you're going to save them. You're going to get your wife back.*

Rik butts in on my newly flowering hope. "Anyway, Ax says he totally gets it," he says. "This kind of stuff is in his blood, he's got psychic relatives going back to Earth-times. I can introduce you."

"Okay, yeah," I absentmindedly respond while composing a reply to Julia 12. "Sure."

"Really? Great! He's the real deal, Dez. I swear."

Whatever, I think.

Shortly after we arrive at the central viewport, a harried woman with short, curly brown hair just slightly darker than her skin comes rushing up the hall with a look in her eyes that says *I'm looking for a strange man with an important message from my sweetheart!*

"Julia!" I call out, feigning confidence.

She looks my way and smiles. "Desmond?"

"Thank you for meeting me."

"Sure thing! What's the message from Sang-Kyu? Is everything okay?"

Technically, no, everything is very bad. "Everything is fine," I lie.

"I know there's no reason you should trust me after I lied about having a message from Sang-Kyu, but I need your help." Her brow furrows like an accordion. "Oh yeah. I was lying. Sorry."

"That's ... okay," she says with her voice, while her body says *get this maniac away from me,* and takes a step back.

"Just hear me out, okay? You can't attack the Anomaly. Aside from having no idea what the consequences will be, my wife is out there and she's never going to take me back if I let her die!"

(Okay, I can tell I'm panicking. I hope that wasn't a bridge too far, I need Julia to help me.)

"It's—" she begins, but I need to make sure she hears my whole plan before she refuses. I should probably come up with a plan.

"Listen, I've got codes that can lock down the local circuitry," I improvise. "But they need to be entered locally. I can give them to you to enter once you're at your console."

"I don't—"

"I know, I know. It's not a permanent solution, but it'll buy us enough time to get Elle and the other researchers back." I've gotten disconcertingly intense, but I'm hoping my passion will sell the plan. "In the meantime maybe we can get SDA on our side."

"Dude!" Julia puts both hands on my shoulders and gives me a shake. "I don't know what you're talking about. Even if you're right, I don't work in weapons…" She trails off thoughtfully. "Wait, are you telling me he's sleeping with Julia from weapons, too? That asshole!"

Stars alive. Does this guy have a Julia fetish or something?

I bring up my LiFESTREAM again. Julias 13 and 14 send back new variations of "Buzz off, weirdo." There are three messages from Julia 15. My heart stops as I read:

> **I'm not sure who this is, but I'm about to head to my shift at weapons. Could you meet me over there? (6 minutes ago)**

> **I'm headed that way now. Let me know if you can meet me! (4 minutes ago)**

> **I've got to clock in now. I'll ping you after. (1 minute ago)**

"I'm sorry, Julia 12," I say. "I've got to run." Surprised that I mean it literally, I turn and sprint towards weapons.

"Dez!" Rik looks up from buffing the viewport. "Where are you going?"

My heart is racing, which makes sense because I'm running for the first time in a year or twenty. My legs and lungs ache. My feet pound the floor and send shivers up to my poorly-cared-for knees. My spirit is in even worse shape than my body. I curse the wide, rounded corridors of the station. Isn't a straight line the shortest distance between two points?

As I retrace my steps through the Th3 NAP, I blink to dismiss the notifications telling me to take another route. *I'll do the work twice,* I think just before I slip on the wet floor. I do a full split and feel something in my thigh tear. (Fine. I deserve that.) With significant difficulty, I pull myself up and limp along.

I come up to the hatch that leads to the weapons sector and key the entry code. After a series of delicate *clicks* and *clanks*, the hatch opens. I step into the long, oblong room. There are rows of workstations, each with a different curvature to make efficient use of space. Running perpendicular to the door, there's an aisle just wide enough to accommodate one person.

The wall opposite the entryway is a mosaic of graphs, charts, and views of the station. The largest screen in the middle displays the Anomaly with a tactical overlay in place. My heart springs a leak. They really are planning to attack the star-cursed thing.

Someone at the front of the room, who must be the commanding officer, looks up as I walk in. Everybody else stays intensely focused on their station. The nervous energy in the room is nauseating. The commanding officer proceeds up the aisle in my direction.

"Excellent Desmond. Apologies if you were misinformed, but we requested not to have this area tended to today. It's a matter of station security. I'll have to ask you to leave."

They must have checked their LiFESTREAM for my name, but I

didn't notice. I check my own for their name. "Excellent Janus, your worship, I only need a minute. I had been talking with Julia about tonight's town hall. I came in to ask her a quick question." I'm hoping that initiating one of us stationers into their cult is more important to Janus than keeping the details of this mission strictly under wraps.

"Well..." Janus looks in what must be the direction of Julia 15's workstation where someone who must be Julia is craning her neck in our direction.

"Ah, I see her right there!" I say, moving in Julia's direction. Taking action during Janus' pause seems to tilt the scales in my favor. They stammer a bit, but seem to settle on letting me stay.

I reach Julia's workstation and, with an amount of difficulty that I'm going to erroneously blame on the pain in my thigh, I take a knee in front of her.

"Hey," I say quietly.

She takes my cue that discretion is paramount and whispers back, "Hey. I don't know who you are."

"I messaged you about Sang-Kyu," I say before adding, "but I don't actually have a message from him."

She gives me a look of pure exasperation. "This is a seriously fucked up day. What is going on?"

"Listen, I need you to help me stop them from attacking the Anomaly."

She starts to speak up, startled that I know about the attack, but I forge onward. "You'd be amazed at the things people will say in front of a janitor. If you're logged into the weapons system, I can give you the emergency codes to cut the circuitry to this whole sector. It's not a permanent solution, but it will buy us some time."

"But—" she begins.

"Listen, I know you could get in trouble. Maybe even lose your job. But do we know what will happen if we attack the Anomaly? And my wife is a researcher. She's out there now. She could get hurt. Even die. I don't want to lose her."

"Dude! You're too late," she says, raising her voice.

I shoot up onto my feet. "What do you mean? Did you talk to Elle? You don't think she'll take me back?" I no longer bother to keep my voice down.

"What? No," Julia says. "I mean, I don't know anything about that! Just … look!" She points at the wall of monitors.

My eyes follow the line implied by her finger and I see the screen she's pointing to. My heart begins to take on water at an alarming rate, claxons blaring and families of blood cells holding each other close.

Time to impact: 00:34:19.

I turn to Janus and say, "What did you do?" Based on the number of people who pry their eyes away from their terminals and look at me with alarm, it's safe to say I bellow it.

"Excellent Desmond, please. There's no need to shout. What seems to be the issue?"

"You're shooting at the Anomaly! That's an issue!"

"We cannot sit idly by as the gates of hell tear open the skin of the universe, which is the surface of the Reflection," they reply with the kind of calm that comes with absolute assurance that you're doing the right thing; that God is on your side.

My outrage fades and I shift to catatonia. When is the next chance I'll have to save Elle's life? This is probably my only shot.

The hatch slides open again. I turn my head expecting, against all reason, to see Elle come through the entryway. Instead, it's Rik.

He scans the room until he finds me. "Dez?"

"They've launched an attack on the Anomaly, Rik. Now I'm never going to get Elle back."

"You and Elle split?" he asks. Maybe I've been too hard on Rik. Of the two pieces of information I just gave him, he zoomed in on that bit?

"Yeah. She told me 18 days ago that she doesn't want to be married anymore."

"Damn."

"Yeah."

"Sorry, dude. I've read you've got 30 to get her back, if that helps."

"Thanks, Rik. I read that too."

I turn and walk back out into the pass with Rik a few paces behind me. He's reduced the bounce in his step to more of a bob. Behind me I hear Janus shout, "I hope you'll still consider joining us at tonight's town hall, Excellent Desmond! I think that you'll find—" before being cut off by the closing hatch.

"Where are you going, Dez?" Rik asks once I've taken a few plodding steps.

"We've still got to polish the viewport, right?"

"Right, but," Rik starts. "Yeah, sure, let's take care of that, buddy." He puts his big slab of an arm across my shoulders, showing me more affection than I deserve.

"It's going to be alright, Dez." Rik says, his arm still acting as a yoke. "I know you think everything seems hopeless now, but…"

I think about the Anomaly while Rik keeps talking, waiting for some kind of retaliation to strike once the bomb makes contact. The masochist in me notes that from the viewport I can at least be witness to the destruction. Then I remember the kindness Rik has shown me in the last few minutes and figure the least I can do is pay attention while he's trying to help.

" …we don't really know shit about the Anomaly," Rik says. "Maybe she'll be okay."

"But if she is, will it be enough that I *tried* to save her?"

"I don't know what happened between you two but, like, did she want a divorce because she thought you wouldn't try to save her if she was in trouble?"

"What does that have to do with anything?" I ask.

"That's what I'm saying, brother."

"No," I reply. "You don't get it. It's complicated."

"Bro, totally. I know," Rik replies. "I wasn't there. I'm just trying to figure out why you saving her was going to fix whatever other problems you were having. Do you think she'll take you back because she feels like she owes it to you? Is that even something you want?"

"I … uh-" I trail off. Did Rik just bring a keen and penetrating emotional insight into our conversation? He's such a meathead. I assumed that everything coming out of his mouth was vapid nonsense.

I take a deep breath and work to puzzle through why Rik is wrong. He has to be wrong, because if he's right–shit. He's right, isn't he?

Stopping the attack wasn't going to make Elle take me back. Good deeds aren't currency. You can't use one to fix another, unrelated problem. How many times had Elle and I had that exact conversation? *Desmond, you cooking dinner doesn't have anything to do with (insert some other issue here).*

"Rik, I've been an idiot."

"It's alright, Dez," he says, giving my shoulders a squeeze. "Happens to the best of us."

It hits me square in the gut: I just want Elle to be okay.

• • •

I pick up a fresh pack of microscrubbers and get to work on my half of the viewport.

Thirty-four minutes and nineteen seconds (apparently) after I learned I was too late, the Anomaly goes dark. Where the pulsing, technicolor whatever-it-is used to be, there's only black with a faint outline of gold dust.

I turn away from the viewport and towards Rik, who's staring at me with his mouth hanging open. I stop myself from internally making a joke about him being a mouth breather—see, people can change—when everything goes pink.

Either the room starts smelling purple and the station is replaced by a field of gold-flecked magenta or something even weirder is happening.

Some internal sense of self tells me that I'm still standing in front of the viewport, but when I try to look around and see if Rik is seeing what I'm seeing, moving my head only causes waves of color to ripple and crash around me, a cacophony of teals and yellows assaulting (what my brain thinks of as) my sense of hearing.

The colors coalesce and shapes form out of the uniformly vibrant void. This is a relief. Being able to sense your body while all of your senses tell you that there is, in fact, no such thing as a body is violently disorienting. But the shapes that are forming don't make any sense. They shift and twist as I look at them, making it impossible to distinguish inside from outside, top from bottom, beginning from end. If I was still sure I had a mouth, I'd worry I was about to puke (which, in turn, would cause more work for me and Rik).

Everything clicks into place and suddenly I'm alone in a version of the station that feels almost right: slightly off, cloyingly colorful but less claustrophobic. I get it now. I'm dreaming. Seems like a weird time to fall asleep, but I have been under a lot of stress.

A body rounds the corner of the pass, headed my direction. It looks … empty? Like a shirt and pants walking about without a body to animate them. The outfit raises an empty sleeve at me and begins to speak.

"Greetings, Eldest Human!"

I look around and don't see anyone else, so I guess that's me.

"Uh, hello," I reply. "What's, um, up?" This is not standard dream fare, so maybe I was wrong. I could be speaking with an alien or maybe the Anomaly is scrambling my brain in response to the attack.

"I have been trying to reach you for some time, Eldest Human!" the outfit says, jovially.

"Listen, I'm not that old, okay? Can we cut the 'eldest' thing?"

"You are the most tenured human in this region," the outfit says. "All who came before you are gone and all others arrived during your reign."

Is that true? I guess I'll take their word for it. "Sure, but there are plenty of old people around here. Like *old* old."

"How do you know they are older than you if they have occupied this space for less time than you have? From their point of view, you have always been here, but from yours, they are newcomers."

"I ... don't know how to answer that," I say. "They say they existed somewhere else before they came here and I choose to believe them about that. Plus, they've got more wrinkles and less hair than I do."

"Interesting," the outfit replies. "Well, we commend your commitment to this place either way. You have paid attention to its cracks and crevices. You have listened and tended to its needs. You are the human with which we wish to speak.

"But we must move on," the outfit continues. "We will have to sort out questions of space and time at a later date. The energy pill you fed us will only produce enough for a short conversation. Introductions. Pleasantries. You can call me Öb."

Energy pill? I think. *That's one hell of a euphemism for a nuclear weapon.*

The outfit, er, Öb, reaches out its non-hand. I reach out and shake the air at the end of its sleeve. There's no need to be rude.

"Desmond. Nice to meet you, Öb. I don't know how to ask this politely: What are you?"

"We are your neighbors!" Öb says, pointing in the direction of the Anomaly, which I now notice is back, floating in its usual place.

"You live in the Anomaly?"

"Yes, let's say that," says Öb. "As I said, I have been trying to reach you for some time, but have had difficulty penetrating the hull of your living quarters and the hull of your consciousness simultaneously."

"So you've been trying to reach me while I sleep," I reply, feeling quite clever.

"Yes! However, with your consciousness turned off, while we can reach you, you don't seem to have much agency. For many years we were at an impasse. We thank you for the pill which gave us the energy needed to push through."

I blink a few times, unsure of where to go next. It doesn't seem wise to explain that, actually, the goal of the bomb was to destroy the Anomaly (and thus, though unknowingly, to destroy Öb).

"Before I depart, I have a request." I nod for Öb to continue. "Certain components of the energy pill are not consumable for us. We would request these components not be included in any future doses."

Öb begins to list off elements and my mind wanders. I'm not a scientist and hopefully, in the future, we won't be so stupid as to fire missiles at the Anomaly.

Something tickles at the back of my brain. Something I'm forgetting.

Dez! Listen, bro! Didn't you just learn this lesson? comes Rik's voice in my head. (Oh stars, is Rik my conscience now?)

"Wait!" I say. "What will happen to these components?"

"We will simply expel them back into your space, where they will dissipate over time."

"No! Please don't!" I say, panicked. "I mean, I don't know what will happen when you do that, but my wife is out there and I'm worried she would be hurt if you returned the energy. Is there any way for you to keep it on your side until we can clear the area?"

"Ah, very well! We do not wish to do harm. We will manage until it is safe."

Our conversation apparently over, Öb holds out their non-hands and, with an inexplicable clap, restores the world back to the one I know. The swirls of color disappear and Rik materializes in front of me, right where I left him, mouth hanging open.

"Dez?" he says. "You don't look so hot."

Everything goes black as I pass out. The absence of color is a great relief.

. . .

I wake some time later in the infirmary. I'm hooked up to an IV (just fluids, nothing fun).

I move my head to scan the room and that's apparently all I've got in me because I feel drained and close my eyes again. I drift in and out and my sleep is quiet and calm, undisturbed by dreams of technicolor halls.

The sixth time I open my eyes, I find Elle sitting in a chair next to my bed. For an instant, I think, *I did it! I saved her and now she'll have to take me back*, but then the part of my brain that's accepted the truth comes online and puts an end to that train of thought. Reality is annoying.

"Elle," I croak.

"Desmond," she replies. "You're awake."

There are a few crumbs of the way she used to look at me in her gaze, but now I'm paying attention instead of defending myself from imagined blame and I see that, more than anything, it's a look of sadness.

"I saved you," I say. "I can't explain it and I wouldn't blame you for not believing me, but I saved you."

"Oh yeah?" she says gently. *Same old Desmond,* she must be thinking. But I'm not supposed to be imagining I know what people are thinking, right? It's a work in progress.

"Yeah. I thought if I saved you, then you would have to take me back."

"That's very Desmond of you."

"I know," I say. "But that's not how things work." I'm embarrassingly proud to have figured that out on my own. (Kind of. I guess Rik helped.)

"I never doubted that you would save me from dying if you could."

"Right. Random acts of kindness can't be substituted for listening to what people actually need."

"I'm glad you figured that out."

"It took a while for me to get there. I'm just glad you're okay."

"I'm glad that you're okay too, Desmond."

"So we're glad all around. That's good. I'm glad." I let my eyes close. "I think I might rest now," I say. Elle probably responds, but I'm asleep before I can hear.

. . .

It's my first shift back at work since the meeting with Öb. The optical scan is still too bright, but nothing else feels the same.

I hear distant sounds of blaster fire. The news that the Emissaries of the Reflection nuked the Anomaly got out and people weren't in love with the idea. They took the bridge while I was unconscious. Now they're rounding up the last of the Emissaries to ship them back to Government Central to be tried for their crimes. It's hostile, but at least it's not an acquisition.

"Dez!" Rik shouts as he walks into the room. "Good to have you back, buddy!"

I turn to look at Rik and am surprised to find myself charmed by his oafishness. I see it now for what it is: unselfconscious enthusiasm. His arms are spread wide as he intrudes on my personal space.

"It's good to be back, Rik," I say truthfully, allowing myself to be folded up into his big bro hug. "What's on the list today?"

. . .

Things I know, in a very specific order:

1. It's safe to assume I know nothing.

2. I know less than I think I do.

3. So, I know less than nothing, I guess?

4. Apparently, I can learn.

* * *

J.P. REYNOLDS is a mathematician and, apparently, a science fiction writer who has had a story published in Daily Science Fiction. He lives in Durham, North Carolina, with his wife and an ever-expanding flock of furry housemates.

www.twitter.com/jpreynlds
www.dailysciencefiction.com/science-fiction/robots-and-computers/j-p-reynolds/mindlessness

Always Become

JASON CLOR

WHEN I COULD move, I unstrapped myself and crawled out of the wreckage. The air was thick with ozone and vaporized coolant. With the electrical storm still raging overhead, I put some distance between myself and the crash site. Only when I could think and see clearly again did I go back to bury Janic.

The wreckage was almost too hot to approach, and his body came free only after a struggle. As I raked a hole in the earth with my bare hands, I told myself, *this wouldn't have happened if Luce had been in that second seat.*

The atmosphere of Ianus 3 was a breathable but volatile stew of thermal inversions and charged ions. Coriolis winds whipped up high-altitude cyclones, and if the solar wind was raging, devastating superstorms could appear with little warning.

Janic had been new … just four months on-world. Qualified to read instruments but unfamiliar with the subtle signs of impending calamity. I hated that he'd never get the chance to learn, and I hated that I'd gotten to know and like him so much.

But none of that meant anything now. All that mattered in the moment was putting him to rest where the planet's native predators couldn't pick him to pieces.

As I placed the last stone atop his body, something inside me shifted. The sudden pain knocked me to my knees, forcing me to unzip my flight suit. Peeling back the blood-soaked undershirt, I discovered a ragged gash along my abdomen. Breathing pushed something purple and distended in and out of that hole.

I won't last long with my innards crawling their way out.

After tearing the sleeves of my suit into strips with my utility knife, I bound my midsection while faerie flashes continued to dance in the squamous clouds overhead. Cramming my guts back inside brought me close to puking. The agony was profound, almost spiritual.

With my abdomen secured and less likely to come undone, I considered the situation. Our hoverlift had suffered a massive lightning strike and come down near the edge of a highland plateau, some 30 kilometers from Frontier Post 113. Directly between the crash site and safety lay a sunken wetland choked with dense foliage and as-of-yet uncategorized fauna, an off-limits region known as Heyford's Slough.

Ranger training called for quick mental calculus. In a situation like mine, the best way to be rescued was to wait near the wreckage. If it was still functional, the craft's emergency beacon would continuously broadcast my location until I was found. But the possibility it had been destroyed was strong.

As I sat surveying the smoking piles of crumpled metal, a tingle teased my neck and cheeks. Before I could process this, the sky erupted with ear-splitting thunder and a blinding flash of searing white. Lances of ten-million-degree plasma pummeled the promontory where I sat, including the hoverlift wreckage. Seconds later, when the assault was over, I found myself face-down in the wet dirt tasting blood.

Bloody hell. Time for Plan B.

Safety, being the first edict of surviving a crisis, required that I abandon the high ground. Persistent wind and atmospheric ionization meant more cluster strikes were likely. Making my way back to 113 along the highland ridges was possible, but might take two days or longer; surviving that long, with my injuries, was far from guaranteed. But I had to try.

The quickest way back, I admitted, *would be to go down into the slough. Down and across and up the other side.*

Then I reminded myself: *a year ago, Luce went down there and never returned.*

She'd wanted something better than a bird's eye view of the curious life forms inhabiting the sunken rifts of Ianus 3. The strange duality of diversity and genetic similarity amongst the planet's myriad organisms had infected her imagination, and she felt her career in the Ranger Corps was stagnating. Restlessness was her life's only constant.

"Don't just be," she'd liked to say. "Always become."

I gazed down the steep slope toward the mist-shrouded tops of pergolas woven of needle-bedecked indigo and carmine branches. Beneath the yowl of the wind tearing through the crags around me, I heard an unearthly chorus of sonorous moans rising from the jungle, accompanied by arpeggios of clicks and crackles. The torrid air rising from below reeked of sweet life and sour decay.

What lured you down there, Luce?

Part of me longed to know. The rest of me was terrified to go.

In the end, was it worth it? Did you find the answers you were looking for?

The pain in my side was spreading like a slow fire. Spurring my numbed legs into action, I found a shallow crevice in the promontory and began to cautiously make my way down into the slough.

· · ·

My hands chafed and bled on the barren stones of the cliff face. As ripples of thunder roiled overhead, I felt utterly exposed, as though the planet was waiting to finish me with one last, smiting blow. Twice, I reconsidered my decision and almost turned back, but as I descended below the tops of the tallest growths in the slough, my surroundings changed radically.

The light of Delta Ianus Aa—a yellow giant slowly devouring its binary partner—faded beneath an interlinked canopy of lace-like fronds and manic corkscrew growths. Foliage—if one could call it that—undulated hypnotically despite an apparent lack of breeze. Through the thickening shadows, my eyes made out minute light sources scattered in all directions.

As I made my way cautiously into that jungle, I felt a mixture of fascination and foreboding; the place was literally alive with movement. Branching stems of translucent blue, fluid-filled and pulsing, recoiled when touched. Helical flowers launched themselves into the air and whirled away. Phosphorescent pods brightened at my approach and dimmed in my passing.

The ground quickly became a sodden stew of mud and organic scum that sucked at my boots, making progress difficult. It felt as though the swamp hid something vast and unwelcoming: an alien consciousness lurking below its surface, testing me, teasing me.

Or maybe … tasting me?

Despite the dizzying variety of organisms I encountered in those first hours, everything in the jungle felt connected. Interlinked somehow.

I was surprised by plant-like things with animalistic behavior, shifting underfoot or stretching out tendrils to touch my face as I walked beneath. Elsewhere were animal-like things rooted in place like mushrooms, twitching and humming, eyes twisting in sockets. The air was thick with fluttering motes … insects? Spores? I covered my nose and mouth with a scrap of cloth and kept moving.

As I recalled from past biotek reports, life on Ianus 3 had long ago retreated from high ground to the lowland canyons and sinks to avoid the planet's deadly wrath. The research genii were just beginning to unlock the secrets of this life's strange genetic code, which—in contrast to the double helix of DNA—was a web-like structure woven with unique protein precursors. Organisms seemed capable of replacing damaged sections of code by patching sections from other sources.

As Luce explained to me once, this meant all Ianus 3 life was closely related, and had probably diversified in rapid bursts many times over the eons. Given such broad variation on shared characteristics, some in the Science Corps wondered if such organisms could even be categorized into species.

"Everything's so new and different," she'd told me, "we barely understand what we're seeing."

"Is that good?" I'd asked.

I remember her face drooping with disappointment. "Of course it is. It's glorious."

Luce hated my need for certainty. For her, mystery was far more enticing, despite the hazards that often accompanied it. The unknown wasn't a danger, but the reason to explore.

"Take a chance and touch the heavens," she'd sing. "Or stay inside and hide from the stars."

It was a quote from her favorite song. And while these were the only lyrics I could recall, in my mind, the melody was as clear as if Luce was humming to me herself.

She was my pole star. I was her anchor.

Sure … just like her, I'd endured decades of induced torpor in order to traverse hundreds of light years for a chance to explore this alien world. But that commitment meant something; I saw no need to recklessly endanger myself—or anyone else—in a blind quest for knowledge.

"The truth is patient," I told her. "It'll still be there when we find it."

But for Luce, risk made discovery all the sweeter. It necessitated hard choices, sacrifices. Change.

So our paths diverged.

By the time I realized the distance between us, I admitted, *it was too late to catch up with her.*

I halted in knee-deep muck and sagged against a large boulder to catch my breath. Its surface was carpeted in silvery strands that vibrated against my skin before retracting into the porous rock. My lungs strained against the heavy, burning sensation filling my chest. Gasping, I watched large, lazy bubbles distend the mud's oily surface, then burst and fill the air with the ripe smell of rot.

As I sat there, a five-limbed creature with a crab-like shell and a crown of eyestalks crept along the ribbed trunk of a towering, arm-shaped frond a few meters away. Though the animal seemed indifferent to me, I couldn't help but feel watched.

It's not this creature, I realized. *The whole place seems to resent my presence.*

The liquid filling my boots was warm and slippery, and the ever-thickening muck clung to my feet and slowed my progress. Walking felt like trying to escape drying cement; with each step, my injury sent pain signals farther and deeper through my body. For a moment, I wondered if my body was starting to fail.

Is this all just an exercise in futility?

My inner pragmatist intervened. *Don't think. There's no time. Just keep moving.*

The terrain in all directions was still flat and choked with foliage. I had no idea how far I'd come, but I knew any hope of crossing the slough would require as much strength as I could summon.

A slow roll of thunder above made me hopeful for rain; by that point, I'd built up an agonizing thirst. Though surrounded by liquid, none of it appeared remotely safe to drink.

Just a few minutes, I told myself. *I'll stand here and catch it in my mouth.*

The shuddering canopy overhead told of a change in the air. Again, the telltale rumble echoed, closer now.

Just enough to kill my thirst.

Less than a minute later, it started to rain. I immediately wished it hadn't.

. . .

Darts of flame lanced through the jungle canopy, shattering the darkness and calm. A barrage of explosive impacts scattered mud, rocks and organic matter high into the air. It took my bewildered brain several seconds to realize what was happening.

The orbit of Ianus 3 intersected the debris trail of a long-missing moon, one pulverized to gravel by some primordial collision. Showers of meteorites fell regularly, but were impossible to forecast without access to instrumentation. And though a sunken jungle was safe from lightning storms, nothing could shield it from this kind of deadly rain.

All around me, the air buzzed with white-hot projectiles. Pulverized fronds and branches crashed down as filthy water splashed upward. I clung to the rock, trying to find solace in the knowledge that my chances of being struck were minuscule.

When that failed, I reassured myself that death by meteor would at least be quick.

. . .

I came awake suddenly, unaware of how long I'd been unconscious.

For one, blissful, disoriented moment, I forgot about my predicament and the shocks of the preceding hours. But then I hauled myself out of the muck; an electrifying sting bisected my torso and brought all the panic and dread flooding back.

While I attempted to regain my bearings within the pulverized landscape, I noticed something remarkable.

My crab-friend was still there, on the trunk of the mammoth frond. A meteor had obviously struck the plant and gouged a great chunk out of its side. And sometime while I was unconscious, the creature had crawled into the hole in the frond and fused with it.

Ignoring my pain for a moment, I sloshed over to the trunk and examined it closely. The substance of the animal's shell had transformed to match the thick, stippled skin of the plant, and one of its limbs had begun to morph into a curled bud from which—I imagined—a new frond would eventually grow.

For a moment, I felt some of the thrill Luce might have experienced had she been there with me.

Glorious.

Moving onward, I noticed similar fusions everywhere, both new and old. And suddenly I had an explanation for the wild hybridizations between flora and fauna. Now there seemed to be a logic behind everything around me, and once I started to see organisms less as individuals and more as sets of components, everything I'd seen began to make a kind of sense.

An entire ecosystem built out of interchangeable parts, I thought. *Remarkable.*

Despite a dizziness brought on by pain and dehydration, I forged on through the mud until I reached a strip of higher ground, where I took a moment to remove and empty my boots. As I was refitting and strapping them with uncooperative fingers, a cold shudder coursed through me and I paused to look around.

As I feared, I wasn't alone.

It crept on stilt-like limbs, deceptively slow, sliding into view through a cluster of segmented cerulean stalks. As dark as a moonless midnight, it seemed formless but for an outline betraying long legs and a tapering snout. Adorning its head were three slitted eyes that burned ember-like and hungry.

The stalking beast's movements conveyed a predatory patience. Once I regained the ability to think, I willed my legs to move me away from that shadow of ill intent.

Along the high ground, I moved as quickly as my faltering feet would carry me. Though I never heard a sound, every time I glanced backward, the beast was there: pinning me like an insect with its luminous eyes, striding with the confidence of a hunter who knows its quarry is stricken and flagging.

Ahead of me lay a thick stand of roots buttressing enormous, bulbous tubers. Hoping this obstacle would prevent the thing from following, I summoned my fleeting reserves and dashed for cover.

This time, I heard the feet of the stalking beast beating the soil behind me. As I lurched into the tangle of hairy roots, the thing slid to a halt, and I could then hear its breath, low and oscillating like a sinister purr. Crawling through the maze with one hand on my side, I gradually put distance between the shadow and myself. When I finally stopped to rest some ten meters deep into cover, I looked back and discovered the thing was gone.

I lay in the dirt for a long time. Condensation from the bulb meters above dripped onto my face, and I caught the drops in my mouth to dampen my thirst. The water was earthy and treacle-sweet on my tongue.

Adrenaline leached out of me, replaced by an astonishing fatigue. I felt leaden, as though I might sink into the dirt and disappear. My brain sent signals to my limbs, imploring them to get up, keep moving … but those signals went nowhere. A sudden chill settled on my skin.

Is this where I end? Frankly, I was hoping for better. Doubt I'm even halfway across the slough. If anyone's looking, they'll never find me down in this muck.

So I rested my eyes, and the eerie sounds of the strange life teeming around me faded. A voice from my past arose from memory.

"Taking risks?" asked the phantom. "It's what we do!"

It was Weinhardt, my ranger instructor. He'd been a jolly man full of colorful anecdotes and a dark sense of humor.

"Taking those risks requires a lot of courage and a little bit of wisdom." He chuckled. "Or is it the other way around?"

Don't talk to me about wisdom, old man. You're back on Earth right now, enjoying retirement.

"Wisdom is knowing what you don't know," Weinhardt said. "A little knowledge can get you into trouble; wisdom will get you out of it."

Save me your empty aphorisms. Talk to me after you've trekked ninety klicks to find only the dead at a crash site. Or, for lack of supplies, helplessly watched a friend die of blood poisoning. Not every tragedy is preventable.

I opened my eyes, expecting the old man to be there, staring down at me with his pearly grin and long beard. Instead, I lay stricken and watched the filtered sunlight fade and take on the grey dullness of dusk.

We take risks. And sometimes they take us.

A shudder passed through me. It seemed to go down into the ground only to be echoed, a small tremor of acknowledgement.

Darkness is coming, I thought. *Let it come.*

Just then, I detected the sound of soft padding. It was enough to jolt me upright; turning to face the sound, I saw a dark silhouette approaching with deliberate care through the tangled roots. My stomach tightened.

This shape was different from that of the stalking beast. It came forward on two legs, tall and straight, unthreatening. Under closer light, it was the color of old skin and new moss, a form riven and reformed with new components, strange growth sprouting from familiar soil.

I had trouble speaking with a dry mouth. "Luce?"

It was her. And it wasn't.

In my current state, there was sufficient reason to doubt what I was seeing … but there she was. Much of her was different. In place of her sturdy arms were scaly tendrils knotted together in an imitation of their original shapes. Gone was the dark hair, replaced by a headdress of glossy thorns. Her skin was a patchwork of old and new flesh, an abstract canvas tinted from the palette of that strange world around us.

But what hadn't changed was devastatingly familiar: her pouting mouth still bewitching, and those milky jade eyes I remembered so well, just as bright … perhaps even brighter than before.

I stood clumsily, trying to make sense of the thing in front of me, as it lifted a hand in a beckoning gesture. When it opened its mouth, I was genuinely terrified of what might come out.

"Let's talk."

. . .

I followed Luce out of the thicket to a clearing of sorts. Tall roots encircled the place, at the center of which was a pool of clear water fed by a trickle from a rocky outcrop. From this I gladly drank, no longer dissuaded by the risk of infection by native microbes.

They'll have me soon enough, I thought.

Swallowing was difficult. I coughed, then regretted it as my side exploded with agony.

"Be still a while," said Luce. It was still a shock to hear her voice, tinged now with melancholy and preternatural calm.

I reclined against a rock and beheld her in the silvery light of sunset. She moved with an uncanny grace, bare feet caressing the ground, body in rhythm with the swell and murmur of the jungle. I tried, for a moment, to work out what had happened to her, how she'd become this chimeric pseudo-Luce; but in the end, I convinced myself that it all might be a fever dream, so the details didn't matter.

When I could comfortably speak, I asked her, "What happened?"

Luce sat at the edge of the pool, dangling her legs in the water, and stared empty-eyed at me for a moment before smiling. It was a strange, rictus grin without the easy charm I remembered. The smile of one who'd forgotten how to be human.

She's been alone a long time, I reminded myself.

"Something," she said. "A terrible moment … an event. Hard. Painful. It separated before from now. I don't remember clearly. Only that I became what I am now."

"What are you?"

"The best part of the person you knew. But also more."

As I contemplated what would encompass Luce's best part, noises distracted me: a clatter of roots, the rush of fallen foliage. I tried to peer through the thicket to their source, but the shadows were already too deep.

"Something followed me here," I said. "It was dark … a predator, I think."

Luce nodded. "I know that one."

"Is it dangerous?"

"Keep away. At all costs."

I shifted to ease my tired bones and my abdomen flared white-hot. Groaning, I pressed my fingers to my side. They came away damp.

"You are dying," said Luce. Her face was beautiful and sad.

I nodded. "Everything dies." And I thought of Janic, lying under stones on the highland.

"Not here!" Her eyes flashed. "Here, the dying find new life. By joining. Something is given and something is taken. A cycle of never-ending."

"I can see what was given to you … but what was taken?"

Those eyes burrowed into me, aglow with unnatural fire in the starlit twilight. "It doesn't matter," she said. "What is taken is replaced. The sum is the same."

Her words carried Luce's passion, but this halting speech was not hers: she'd always been the more articulate of the two of us. *How much of that brain is still hers?*

"You came here for a reason," she said, leaning toward me.

Even before she opened her mouth to explain, I already knew what she was suggesting. And my head was shaking no.

"I look at you," I said, "and I'm afraid."

"Don't be," she whispered. "I am happy. And I will keep you safe. Here in the peaceful place. Safe."

My dying mind welcomed the idea of remaining with Luce, in memory … but not the way she meant. Together as in the past, a broken relationship rebuilt from the fragments of two lives. Isn't that what heaven should be?

But not by this joining. Not by being taken apart. Death, I could accept. But not losing myself.

And safety? That's not my Luce.

"When you left to come here…," I said, "…when you didn't come back, I had to let you go. What we had before, we'll never get back. Let me remember you as you were."

She shook her head. "Before doesn't matter."

"Always become," I said, and I couldn't help smiling. But her face had a look of incomprehension.

So I tried again. "You don't want to hide from the stars."

"You speak strange words," she whispered.

"Your words."

Her head shook once, twice. The gesture was a protest, a rejection.

"One time," I said, "we shared these words. They belonged to both of us. A symbol of our bond."

"Words," she muttered. "Just pieces. Interchangeable."

Something caught in my throat and I gagged. The reflex turned into a cough, and reminders of my dire state radiated outward from my wound. As I lay there, wrapped in a blanket of pain, a distant sound cut in from above, sharp and insistent. *A hoverlift?*

I lifted my hand to point. "There … are they looking…"

Luce stroked my face with twig-like fingers. "They will never find us here."

Then she bent and kissed me. Her cold, unfeeling lips tasted of disuse, sediment, decay.

In that moment, I realized: Luce was dying too.

It was felt in the need she expressed, in the hunger of her grip on my arm. The alien DNA was rejecting the human parts of her; that's why she needed me. To be whole again.

Where were you when I needed to be made whole?

The enormity of her desire in the face of my own mortality struck me like an electric shock. I rolled away from the pool and onto my hands and knees. A splash told me she had risen to follow.

"Let me help you."

Somehow, I found my feet. The clearing, the jungle, and the sky were spinning. At first, all I could do was breathe. Waves of pain and fever pulsed through my chest and skull. Luce stood glaring two paces away, her swamp-body glistening.

The body remains, I thought. *But the soul is gone.*

I had to leave. To save the part of me that longed to stay.

I said, "No."

Her eyes goggled and I recoiled. Then her head tilted back and from her mouth erupted an inhuman keening. The sound shook me to the core; I clapped my hands over my ears to try to shut it out. Then, feeling my insides begin to revolt, I staggered away, back toward the thicket of roots.

The shriek was followed by sounds I cannot describe: guttural shouts, like syllables of some tongue unspoken for eons. I got the impression she was cursing me … or rather, *something* was cursing me, from across a gulf of time, through her lips.

Too late, love. Too late.

She did not follow. Perhaps the pool was all that was keeping her alive. Perhaps primal rage prevented her from reacting. I crashed into the thicket blindly, away from the alien sound of her, that twisted phantom of Luce. Any fate was better than surrender to a dead dream.

Woozy and disoriented, I stumbled out into a moonlit patch of soil. Something slithered away from the intrusion of my footsteps. A blanket of mist rose from the nearby bogs, robbing the ground of its reality.

And there, in the shadows, was the stalking beast. Waiting.

It came forward silently, like a piece of the night itself. With no strength left to stand, I sank to my knees. A hush seemed to fall over the jungle. Or my heart was in my ears. The creature's eyes were the apertures of a lantern, ablaze with amber fire.

Behind me, the shouting had died away. Numb with fever and exhaustion, I waited. Breathing heavily, searching for air. Then a sound forced me to stop and listen.

High and lilting, notes fell softly like midnight snow. Notes to a song I knew by heart.

Luce's song.

The stalking beast inched toward me, humming this gentle lullaby.

To me. For me. At last, a swell of tears flooded my eyes.

Something is given. Something is taken.

Slowly, within the beast's shadow, a mouth appeared. Its teeth were like cut glass, its breath hot.

The sum is the same.

With my last bit of strength, I reached up to put my arms around the shadow.

Always become.

* * *

JASON CLOR is a writer living in Portland, Oregon, USA, where he dabbles in science fiction, fantasy, horror, and the occasional comic book. He is currently finishing a three-novel cycle set in the distant future. When not in front of a keyboard, Jason enjoys photography, board games, cocktails and making pizza. His cats played no part in writing this bio.

www.jasonclor.com